# THE CHANGE

# GUY ADAMS

D0239444

First published 2017 by Solaris
an imprint of Rebellion Publishing Ltd,
Riverside House, Osney Mead,
Oxford, OX2 0ES, UK

*www.solarisbooks.com*

ISBN: 978 1 78108 583 7

10 9 8 7 6 5 4 3 2 1

A CIP catalogue record for this book is available
from the British Library.

Designed & typeset by Rebellion Publishing

Printed in the UK

# NEW YORK
## THE QUEEN OF
## CONEY ISLAND

Outside the cabin, she heard her uncle screaming and wondered if today was to be the day she would die.

# Chapter One

**Eight Months Later**

'THE QUEEN WILL fix it,' the old man said. 'Ain't nothing on the river she don't handle.'

He poked at the contorted body of the stray cat he was roasting on his campfire, spat into the flames laced with burning plastic and singed fur, and offered a smile that proved his dinner was going to be hard to chew.

'The alternative is to go it without permission,' he continued, 'but I don't recommend it. Last I heard, The Fishermen were eating anyone who floated past without the Queen's say so.' He smiled again. 'And don't think they don't have a taste for dark meat, they'll put anything in their cooking pots.'

Grace squirmed, as much at the reference to her ethnicity as the thought of feeding cannibals. The world had ended and here was someone who thought it important to point out she was African American.

'Talking of food,' said the old man, lifting the hissing carcass from the fire, 'I don't mind sharing if you don't mind keeping me company.' That smile again. all purple gums and breath that made your eyes water. 'I don't mind a little dark meat either.'

Racist and willing to sleep with kids. What a great city this was.

'I'm fifteen,' she said.

He shrugged as if the information was meaningless to him. No doubt it was.

'World's moved on,' he said, 'nothing matters anymore.'

She left him to his meal, thankful that he was too weak to stop her.

# Chapter Two

THAT NIGHT SHE slept on the back seat of a car beneath Shore Parkway. Most people avoided the cars because of the dead bodies they often contained but Grace didn't like to sleep in the open. If she found an empty backseat she'd take it, turning her back on any dry remains left upfront. What was one more dead body in a world filled with them? The dead could only hurt those that had loved them, to anyone else they were street furniture.

As she was dropping off she heard the sound of gunshots coming from Coney Island Hospital. She pulled her coat over her so that anyone looking through the dirty window would see nothing but a lifeless bundle on the backseat. The hospitals and medical centres had become dangerous places, a target for those looking for drugs or weapons. A way to kill yourself or someone else. Let them get on with their business.

In sleep she returned to the cabin. The darkness that had seemed oppressive for the first couple of weeks then a security blanket as the world outside became a place to hide from. She remembered the smell, the splinters beneath her fingernails, the stomach cramps of hunger. She remembered the way the moonlight would catch on the metal bars, little pieces of freedom to remind her of what she'd lost. She remembered Uncle Ray, his dead body bloating and then thinning out once more. A flux of flesh followed by grinning bone.

A couple of hours later she was woken by screaming in the road behind her. She was tempted to stay wrapped up and hidden but curiosity got the better of her. She peered through the back window to see a woman being chased by a man in a white lab coat. The woman was unsteady, trailing plastic tubing and plastic sacks from cannulas in her hands. The man was whooping with excitement, in no hurry to catch her as she weaved between the cars. The woman stumbled and fell to the road. The man opened his lab coat to reveal stained underwear and a selection of instruments taped onto his body. Metal glinted in the moonlight. Grace wrapped herself up and tried to go back to sleep; the things she saw there weren't much better but at least they were familiar. Despite the screaming, she eventually managed.

# Chapter Three

MORNING POURED ITSELF over the freeway and Grace woke to stiff bones.

She glanced around to make sure the coast was clear then climbed out, stretched and wondered about breakfast. She ate a vacuum-packed pastry, washing it down with bottled water and continued the final stretch towards the coast.

She didn't look up at the intersection, the bodies hanging from the lights were just like all the rest. They creaked on their ropes, the gentle breeze swinging them to and fro. A sign painted on the road told her SO ALL SINERS MUST PAY.

To her left stood a tenement block with a crenellated roof. Flags flew from its summit, bright colours whipping against a murky sky.

'What ho, girl,' called a voice in a thick Bronx accent, 'how goes the day?'

She looked for the speaker, finding him stood to the side of one of the flags. An elderly man wearing an improvised suit of metal oven trays and a motorbike helmet with the visor removed.

'OK,' she replied, 'you?'

He shrugged with a clatter. 'Nobody's tried to kill us yet.'

'Then it's a good day.' She made to carry on.

'Mind yourself on the corner of Ocean View,' the voice called after her, 'God's been in a lousy mood all week.'

It had been longer than that in Grace's opinion but she waved her thanks and continued on her way. A few seconds later she heard the flat blast of a trumpet as the old man greeted the rest of the street in his own, crazy manner.

She rummaged in her backpack for something else to eat, pulling out a bruised apple. Carefully eating around the brown flesh, she drew closer to the intersection with Ocean View Avenue.

Just ahead, there came the sound of breaking glass. She moved to the other side of the street, wanting to give herself room to run should she need it. The glass was followed by the sound of pounding metal. As she came opposite the Guardian Angel church she spotted a man with long, white hair and beard stood on top of a parked car, pounding it with a sledgehammer. He was wearing colourful priest's robes, shining purple and black silk.

'Damn you!' he roared as he took another swing at the car, 'and coming from me you know that means something!'

This, Grace presumed, was God. As he spun around on the car roof, the beard, false now she saw it from the front, slipped slightly and he breathed a mouthful of it in, choking. Panicking, he lost his balance and fell off the roof, the sledgehammer toppling from his hands. The air filled with the sort of cursing deities were generally thought to frown upon.

Grace circled around, not wanting to be seen. She was out of luck.

'Hey kid!'

She stopped moving, looking over to where God had fallen, his robes hiked up to reveal spotted boxer shorts and socks pulled up by suspenders.

'Give an old deity a hand, for Christ's sake!' he shouted.

She considered running; it obviously showed.

'Come on!' he pleaded, 'I'm God! If I wanted to hurt you I could smite you from here. I'm a beneficent deity, one whose robes are caught in the door of this damned Nissan.'

'Then magic them unstuck,' she suggested.

'And cheat you of the chance to help the Lord? What sort of miserable God would do a thing like that? Please kid, the blood's rushing to my head here, things are looking even weirder than normal.'

She thought about it for a moment and then moved over to help him.

'Bless you,' he said as she tugged at his snagged robes, 'there'll be a bounty for you in Heaven. Coffee in the vestry too if you want.'

Grace decided she did. God didn't seem interested in harming her and she wouldn't mind asking him what he knew about the Queen. The more she knew what to expect, the better.

'Why were you smashing the car?' she asked him as they entered the church.

'Keeps me fit,' he replied.

The vestry was a clutter of books, unwashed plates and crates of food. She looked through his supplies. God had a sweet tooth it seemed: bars of chocolate and bags of candy. At the centre was a table and chairs, buried under spilling piles of newspapers.

'If you're hungry,' said God, 'help yourself.'

He stared at her in a manner that he no doubt thought of as intimidating. With the beard, the effect was compromised. 'Don't think I didn't notice you were eating an apple earlier. Apples are bad for you.'

'I'm fine thank you,' she told him, 'but the coffee would be great.'

He shrugged and began to hunt for a clean cup.

'So where are you headed?' he asked her, rinsing a cup and drying it with his beard.

'I want to see the Queen,' she told him, doing her best not to think about the state of the cup her coffee was being poured into. 'I need to get to Rikers Island.'

'I knew that of course,' he said, though the look of shock on his face proved his omnipotence false. 'And I also know why you'd want to do such a stupid thing. Still, it would be good for you to get it off your chest so let's just pretend I don't and you tell me anyway.'

'I'm trying to find my brother,' she told him. 'He was there before... before everything happened.'

He nodded. 'The Change,' he said, 'that's what they call it.'

'Yeah.'

He handed her the coffee and poured one for himself. He sipped at it for a moment, adding to the dark stains in the hair around his mouth.

'It's been a long time,' he said, 'what makes you think he's still there?'

'I don't know where else to look.'

'Where were you when it happened?' he asked.

'My Uncle Ray's.'

'And you didn't see anything?'

'I was ill. Measles. Couldn't open my eyes. Light burned.' Which was an out and out lie, albeit one based on a truthful memory. She'd had measles a few years before and remembered the blinding pain at its height.

'A miracle,' he said, bowing his head slightly as if expecting thanks. 'And after. On the news or the Internet?'

She shook her head. 'The power was out.'

'Because you know that some videos of it leaked. They're dangerous. Looking at it second-hand wouldn't kill you, not like it did for those that were there, but it has... power.'

She knew this of course. Hadn't she seen its effect on her Uncle Ray? She had no intention of discussing it, though, no more than she planned on telling him where she'd really been when The Change had hit.

'I didn't see anything.'

'That's good,' he said, 'because some people that saw it...' his face took on a dreamy quality, 'they were affected quite badly. Not me of course, I could handle it, being God and everything, but some people... they went completely nuts.'

'What was it like?' she asked him. 'I mean, I've heard stories. The things in the sky. The shadows...'

He shook his head. 'It's best not to talk about them. They're ungodly. They came and broke my world. People pray, they ask me why I... why I would... But it wasn't me. This was nothing to do with me.'

He was getting agitated and Grace was concerned he might turn nasty.

'I know,' she said, touching his arm, 'you'd never have done something like that.'

He nodded, his coffee spilling slightly. 'I mean, they talk about the flood but that was different. I had to do that, things had gotten... complicated, but this? No. Not me.'

'Of course not,' she repeated, 'let's sit down for a bit. You can tell me about the Queen.'

The change of subject seemed to help. 'The Queen?'

'Yeah, you know, what should I be careful of?'

He laughed and, just like that, his mood changed. 'Just about everything! I mean, seriously, that woman's mad!'

He sat at the table, shunting a stack of the *New York Times* out of the way so he could put his coffee down.

'She's running most of Coney Island,' he said, 'and as far as I'm concerned she's welcome to it. You've seen what's happened to some places? The way they've been changed?'

'Not much,' she admitted. 'I stayed where I was for a few months.' She pictured the cabin. The slow scraping at the floor to get free. 'I've heard from other people on the road though,' she said, 'it's not just the people who died or went mad.'

'It's the city itself. All cities probably. Everywhere. The very earth has changed. People used to say that ghosts were just symptoms of history and emotion getting soaked up into the bricks and mortar of the real world. As if the world could become infected by what happened on it. It was true. So many places are now... I don't know, they've become as screwed up as everything else.'

'And Coney Island is like that?'

'It always was a place of dreams. I've not been there, not because I'm scared of course, I'm God, what could harm me?'

*A battered Nissan car*, thought Grace.

'Still,' he continued, 'I've heard enough about the place from people who have. I really don't think you should go.'

'If I want to get to Rikers, the river is the only way, you can't get through Queens anymore. I tried. But if I don't get permission...' She let the thought hang there.

He nodded. 'You do what you have to do,' he said. 'That's always been God's way; I don't like to interfere. Bear in mind though that means I can't intercede on your behalf. Not even if things get really screwy.'

'I understand.'

'It's nothing personal, just the rules you know? I'll walk some of the way down with you though, even God sometimes needs to stretch his legs.'

# Chapter Four

GOD PUT ON a pair of lopsided Ray-Bans and headed onto Ocean Parkway with Grace. Resting on one shoulder was his sledgehammer in case 'I need to do any smiting on the way.'

Coney Island was a short walk through Brighton Beach and Grace partly wished God had let her carry on alone. She would have moved quicker and been less obvious. Still, in a world where any kind of charitable thought was rare, she shouldn't complain when someone tried to be nice.

'How come you lived with your uncle?' he asked her as they made their stately way through Brighton Beach.

'My parents died when I was a baby. 9/11. My brother and I were shuffled around the family until they could find somewhere we could stick. Brett's ten years older than me. It hit him harder. He knew them, I never did. He went his own way.'

'And ended up in prison.' He didn't make it sound judgemental but Grace was always defensive on the subject.

'He couldn't help it.' She didn't really believe this more than anyone else but couldn't help but defend him. 'He made bad choices.'

'We all do sometimes.'

She waited for him to ask what crime Brett had committed, people usually did, but he stayed silent, just shifted his sledgehammer from one shoulder to the other.

'It doesn't matter anymore,' she said, 'with all this. Who cares? I need to find out if he's ok. He's probably the only family I have now.'

'He was in a better place than most when it comes to surviving,' he said. 'He probably didn't see Them. I hope you find him.' He seemed to remember who he was supposed to be. 'Of course, I know he's alive really. I'm God. I know everything. So have hope, all will be well. Probably. Bearing in mind any accidents caused from your having free will and everything.'

It was nonsense but he meant well.

'Thank you,' she said, her attention drawn by a group across the road. They were gathering around a three-level, red brick building, chanting and waving a selection of weapons in the air. Baseball bats, chains, someone fired a handgun.

'I don't like the look of that,' God admitted, 'some sort

of mob. Yes, definitely a mob. Probably the Russian mob in fact, you know what Brighton Beach is like.'

They kept to the other side of Ocean Parkway, using the cars for cover.

'I wish I could just wipe them from existence,' God said, 'but I can't abuse my powers, that wouldn't be right.'

Now they were directly across from the crowd, they could hear what they were chanting.

'Baba Yaga?' Grace repeated, 'what's that mean?'

'Russian for I'm going to hit you with my baseball bat,' said God with misplaced confidence. 'No doubt someone inside the building has got on their wrong side, let's just get out of here shall we?'

Grace had no problem with that but, as they continued to move between the cars, the air was filled with the sound of crumbling masonry and the building the Russians had been gathered around rose slowly into the air.

'That's just not right,' said God, shaking his head in disbelief.

'How's it doing that?' Grace wondered, trying to see through the trees and the crowd to get a clearer view of the building.

There was a a loud cheer from the crowd as the building tilted from side to side and then moved forward. The cheer turned into screams of panic and Grace finally got a clear view. Emerging from the base of the building were two scaly pairs of legs, like those of a chicken. Its taloned feet slammed down on the people that, moments ago, had been praising it. The air filled with screams and cracking bones as the building pushed through the trees and out into the road.

'I think you should run,' said God. 'I shall stay here and fight it. I am God after all.'

He raised his sledgehammer and made to run into the road but Grace grabbed him. 'That would be an abuse of your powers,' she said. 'I'd much rather you just ran as well.'

'If you think it best,' he said, and sped off ahead of her, sprinting towards the ocean.

# Chapter Five

THEY KEPT TO the side of the road as the walking building continued to totter around on its spindly legs. The Russians had quickly switched from adoration to panicked defence. Shots rang out, bullets piercing the building's windows and ricocheting of its bricks.

With luck, Grace thought, running past God, the mobsters and the building would keep each other occupied until they were out of sight.

Sadly, as the ocean came into view, she heard the heavy feet pounding down the road towards them; a mad, witch-like cackle cutting through the air. Just ahead of them was a large barricade built from wooden sheeting, sandbags and barbed wire.

Above the barricade a colourful sign, painted in swirling reds and blues announced The Queendom of Coney Island. If only they could reach it in time they might be safe.

'Faster!' she shouted to God, looking back over her shoulder. 'We're nearly there!'

'Baba Yaga!' the cackling voice called and she could see the face of an old lady at one of the upper windows, leaning out over the sill, long grey hair whipping around her head.

God turned to look. His sledgehammer slipped from his hands and he tripped over it as it clattered to the ground. With a yell he fell on his back in the middle of the road, staring up at the advancing building. Any moment now, he would be stepped on and all pretence of his being the Almighty would be smeared across the tarmac.

She considered leaving him, just another dead body in the road, but she couldn't do it. However much the last few weeks had made her numb to the death of strangers, she couldn't stand by and see someone who had been kind to her die, not if there was anything she could do to help.

She picked up the sledgehammer, and did her best to wave it over her head. It was so heavy she ended up doing little more than shaking it ineffectively. She roared at the top of her voice and ran towards the building's legs, hoping she could move quickly enough to avoid them as they shuffled and stamped their indentation into the surface of the road.

God rolled out of the way just in time to avoid being crushed; the three-toed foot clenching, its talons digging thin wounds in the road.

Grace swung the sledgehammer down on the foot, pleased to hear a rewarding crack of thin bones as the hammer did its damage.

Above them, the old woman roared with rage and the building toppled precariously, its damaged foot rising into the air as it tried to avoid a second blow.

Grace was already running towards the second foot, swinging the sledgehammer again. This time the foot darted away from her, trying to avoid suffering the same fate as its partner. It was an automatic reaction and one that robbed the building of its balance.

The old woman screeched in anger and panic as her home stumbled backwards, hopping and shuffling as it tried to avoid falling over.

'Run!' Grace shouted, dropping the sledgehammer and making for the barricade, snatching at God's robes as she passed.

'I don't want to go in!' he shouted. 'I'm God, I'll be fine out here.'

'No you won't!' she replied, banging on the barricade. 'Hey! Let us in! There's a monster house out here trying to kill us!'

Behind them, the building had retreated some distance but it was regaining its balance and she was sure that it would soon resume its attack.

She banged on the barricade again. 'Come on! We're here to visit the Queen!'

A hatch slid back and she found herself staring into a water tank, a large fishy eye staring back.

'Hi,' she said, rather hesitantly. 'Can we come in?'

Another hatch slid back, this one revealing a speaker grill. 'What do you want?' asked a deep voice, distorted by the water. The tank in front of her filled with bubbles as the eye's owner spoke.

'We want to come in,' she said again.

'Speak up,' the aquatic voice said. 'I can't hear you.'

'We want to come in!' she shouted.

'Why?'

'To see the Queen.' She stepped to one side. 'And to get away from that.'

The eye stared out of the tank, looking at the building that was now making its way back towards them, limping slightly thanks to its damaged foot.

'House on legs,' the voice said. 'Weird.'

'So let us in!'

'What's the password?' the voice asked.

'I don't know!'

'Wasn't talking to you.' Another hatch slid back, a couple of feet higher and to the right of the first. In this one she could see the bloated, scaled face of something that resembled a puffer fish crossed with a baby.

'Can't remember,' said a new voice. 'Something to do with cotton candy I think. Or do I mean baboons?'

'Baboons?' Grace shouted in exasperation.

'That must be it,' said the new voice. 'Baboons are definitely to do with baboons. Let her in.'

'You sure?' asked the first voice. 'I think she was just guessing.'

'Baboons are not the sort of thing you randomly guess,' said the second voice. 'You're being paranoid again. Let her in.'

'If you're sure.'

A hatch large enough to walk through appeared and Grace dragged God inside.

'What about the building with legs?' the first voice asked as they entered a dark tunnel.

'Does it know the password.'

'It keeps screaming "Baba Yaga".'

'That has absolutely nothing to do with cotton candy. Or baboons. Or anything really. Tell it to go away.'

'I don't think she'll listen,' said Grace. It was lighter now and she could see that they were in one of those glass tunnels they had in big aquariums, the sort where you could walk through the large tanks and see the fish swimming around you.

Looking back she could see the other side of the barricade, the fish people floating in front of the barricade windows watching the advancing building.

'Cannon?' asked the one that looked like a puffer fish.

'Cannon,' the other agreed, a more slender creature, elongated arms and legs poking out of an algae-covered track suit. Its eyes were huge and jutted from either side of its narrow head.

A long, black cylinder sat between them, attached to the barricade. The puffer creature bobbed over to it and pulled a stout lever on its side.

There was a deep boom and the water fizzed around them as the cannon sucked and then expelled some of the tank's contents. In the distance, muffled from their position inside the tunnel, Grace heard a dull crump as the jet of water hit its target. A moment later there was a crashing sound.

'What's a Baba Yaga then?' asked the puffer creature.

'Blowed if I know,' its partner replied, 'but it's lying outside with a pair of broken legs.'

'Don't suppose it really matters then.'

The puffer creature swam down to Grace and God, pressing its face up against the glass of the tunnel. 'You two had better follow me.'

# Chapter Six

THEY WALKED ALONG the tunnel, the puffer creature bobbing along beside them on the other side of the glass.

'Amazing how you knew the password,' it said, its voice echoing through the tunnel from speakers set at intervals on the roof. 'Mind you, everyone always seems to. They give us hell about it somedays. "Foogs," they say, "you'll let anybody in."'

'Foogs?' asked Grace, 'that's your name?'

'I suppose so,' Foogs replied, 'otherwise they're all just being weird. Who's the guy in the dress?'

'I am God,' God replied, 'and I've fed multitudes on things like you so watch your mouth.'

'Good luck with that pal,' said Foogs. 'One lick of me and you'd be dead.'

'Don't mind him,' said Grace, 'he's in shock.'

'I'm not in shock,' God replied. 'I'm just feeling wrathful.

I never wanted to come in, I was only going for a walk.'

'Better this than stay outside,' she told him.

'Tell me that again when the Queen's sawing your head off to use as a bowling ball.'

Around them, reeds rippled and rock formations towered. Aquatic creatures dashed to and fro. An eel with a woman's face followed them for a short way, her Hollywood smile parting to reveal needle teeth. A turtle with human hands in place of its legs pulled itself along the roof of the tunnel, the wrinkled palms slapping a rhythm as it passed over them towards the barricade.

Grace supposed The Change had worked its peculiar magic on the New York Aquarium, extending it out beyond its walls and filling the water with creatures no visitor had ever clapped their eyes on. As she watched, a dolphin with a Mohican haircut chased a shoal of eyeballs against the glass of the tunnel; they pattered against the side, bouncing off in the opposite direction like rubber balls.

'What's the Queen like?' she asked Foogs.

'Pink,' he replied, 'and remarkably dry.'

Which wasn't much help really.

'Is she dangerous?'

'Not to me, your mileage may vary. It depends on her mood. Why do you want her?'

'I need to get to Rikers Island.'

'Ah... once upon a time that would have been easy, all

you had to do was shoot someone in the head. I hear it's more complicated now. If she likes you, she'll help.'

'And if she doesn't?'

'She won't.'

'Will she kill us?'

'Why would you want her to do that?'

'I don't.'

'Don't ask such a silly question then, she might think you're serious and before you know it you're a regular breath away from continued existence. If I were you kid, I'd be more careful how you express yourself. Anyway, you'll soon find out. This is as far as I go.'

Ahead of them was another large barricade, the tunnel finishing in a small doorway.

'Give her my love if you see her,' said Foogs, darting off. 'Actually better not, she has no idea who I am, it'll only confuse her.'

Grace looked at God, he shrugged, so she placed her hands on the door and pushed.

# Chapter Seven

'GIVEN THE NATURE of my existence,' said God as they stood on the other side of the door taking in their first glimpse of the place Coney Island had become, 'it is very hard to surprise me. I mean, omniscience can really take the joy out of things. Still, if I wasn't omniscient I'd be having a nervous breakdown around now. If you want to throw up or anything I'll quite understand but try and avoid the robes. And the sandals.'

'I'm fine,' said Grace. And she was; she had begun to worry over the last couple of weeks that something inside her had permanently snapped. Her ability to feel fear, wonder, sympathy for the dead... every emotion felt dialled right back to the point of barely existing. She knew that a therapist would tell her she was still in shock, that there was only so much tragedy someone could experience before their mind just went quiet, shut itself away and refused to engage. Maybe that was true. If so, in absolute honesty, it had happened long before The Change, but she supposed it was a possible explanation for the empty feelings inside her.

That aside, looking out on the streets around them, she did feel a distant, familiar sensation that might well have been awe.

The lavishly painted sign she'd seen on the barricade was a drab precursor to the world it promised. Everything was painted, the buildings, the sidewalk, the road; an alternating fairground-bright mix of reds, blues, yellows and greens. Doors clashed with brickwork which clashed with fairy lights strung around the windows. Banners and balloons were strung from the roofs and streetlights, some advertising shows and performers; others just offering paintings of happy faces, clowns, leaping dolphins and motorbikes hurtling through fiery hoops.

The air was filled with conflicting smells, a sideshow perfume of fried food, ozone, sweat, petrol, sawdust and manure. Even the steady breeze coming in off the sea couldn't dispel it.

The noise was just as chaotic, shouting, revving engines, blaring klaxons. Countless pieces of music fought one another for attention, booming classical horns butted against thrash guitars with pounding dance basslines thudding between the two.

It was enough to make your brain creep down your throat and try to hide in your stomach.

None of which took into account the actual people that called Coney Island home. At first glance, many of them seemed perfectly normal but for their outlandish clothes (everything from ballgowns to space suits) but closer inspection revealed the more unconventional genes that surrounded them. The creatures in the aquarium had contained some human DNA but, for the most part, had still been fish; here the distinction was far less obvious. A man in a purple bowler hat and a black and white check leotard walked by swishing a lion's tail behind him, the furry tip bobbing along in time with the music he was listening to through a large pair of headphones.

A pair of conjoined twins danced past, their cheerleader outfits enhanced by flashing lights from a Christmas tree.

A man with a long beard of frilly skin skied through the crowd on a pair of skateboards. Every now and then he poked those he passed with the tip of his ski poles, shouting instructions for people to clear out of his way.

Grace felt someone tug at the leg of her jeans and she saw a small child whose body turned into that of a spaniel below the waist. The child scratched behind her ear with a hairy back leg and looked up at Grace with an exaggerated look of sadness.

'Got any smokes?' she asked.

'I don't,' Grace replied.

'To hell with you then,' the girl replied, trotting off in search of someone else to ask, her palms slapping on the road.

'This,' said God, 'is a ridiculous place. On reflection I rather like it.'

'It could be worse,' Grace admitted, 'at least nobody seems very interested in us.'

They walked through the crowds, taking in sight after sight.

There was a roar of approval as the air filled with a loud twang and a man with paper wings was catapulted high into the sky, landing some seconds later in the distant ocean. No doubt he was quite dead by the time he hit the water but he had seemed quite happy with his fate, his laughter trailing behind him along with his false wings.

'If I'd meant man to fly...' God muttered but didn't comment further.

'Where do you think the Queen is?' Grace asked.

'I can't interfere, remember,' he replied, 'though if I were you I'd be aiming towards that castle.'

Grace could see the brown and yellow towers poking up in the distance. They were painted as if from a cartoon, the sort of castle talking animals frequented.

As they drew closer they realised it wasn't painted, it was plastic. An inflatable, bouncy castle the size of a small building. Thick chains held it in place, though the towers swayed from side to side, the guards that stood atop of each hanging on for dear life as their vantage point shifted back and forth with every step.

At the main entrance a ticket booth had been erected

with a handprinted sign saying 'Appointments to see the Queen'. Below it, a blackboard featured hand-written times of day, like announcements for an animal show at the zoo.

Grace looked at her watch. 'First appointment time isn't until two o'clock,' she said, 'that's hours away.'

God walked up to the booth which was inhabited by a pair of albino girls in chainmail.

'We'd like to see the Queen,' he said.

The girls were reading an old copy of the *National Enquirer*, cooing over claims and stories that now seemed tame in a world post-Change.

One of them extended a pointed finger towards the blackboard as they continued to read in silence.

'Yes,' said God, 'I saw that. Are there no exceptions?'

'No exceptions. No minors. No-one below the legal height will be admitted,' said the girl who had pointed, her extended finger now veering over towards a wooden cut-out of a pirate that stood to the right of the booth. 'Measure up against Black Roger to see if you make the grade.'

'I don't think that'll be necessary. Are you sure we couldn't get in sooner?' The girl who was speaking now stared at him in silence. 'Fine. No exceptions. Do we need to book?'

'First come first served,' she replied. 'Get here early to beat the lines.'

'It's popular then?'

'Not very,' she admitted, 'just a few weirdoes and loons. Get here fifteen minutes before we open and you'll be golden. Though not literally. If you want miracles she only performs those at weekends.'

'Part timer,' he muttered, returning to Grace. 'We need to kill time for a few hours, they're not letting us in.'

Grace looked around. 'I suppose there's plenty to see.'

God straightened his beard and brushed imaginary dust from his robes. 'Well, stick close, who knows what sort of maniacs we might bump into.'

Grace rolled her eyes. 'I was about to say the same thing to you,' she replied, walking off ahead.

# Chapter Eight

THEY STOPPED FOR a while to watch a One Man Band. Rather than the usual assortment of strapped percussion, he controlled a veritable orchestra of instruments. He was helped in this by the unusual quantity of limbs he possessed. Feet stomped on bellows that huffed air into brass and woodwind, fingers pulled bows across stringed instruments and, in the middle, he alternated between singing and head-butting a kettle drum.

He was halfway through a version of Teenage Kicks when he came to an abrupt halt and fell asleep, his face pressed against the drum. The skin quivered as his snores reverberated through the belly of the instrument.

'Guess the show's over,' said Grace, leading them away from the sleeping musician.

In the distance they could see the familiar spiral tracks of the Cyclone roller coaster.

'Ever been on it?' Grace asked God.

'God does not do roller coasters.'

'He does today.'

They worked their way over to the Cyclone, stopping briefly to take in the sight of a large woman juggling fish. Every now and then she allowed one to drop into a bucket of water between her feet, a pedal flipped the refreshed fish back into play and, one by one, they continued to spin.

'How come she's singing but her lips don't move?' asked Grace.

'It ain't the woman that's singing,' God replied, 'it's the fish.'

Arriving at the Cyclone they were surprised to be greeted by a man wearing evening dress.

'Table for two?' he asked.

'We just want to ride the roller coaster,' Grace replied.

'Naturally,' the man said, smiling without an ounce of sincerity. Above his crumpled upper lip a drawn-on moustache began to smudge. 'Table for two?'

'Yes,' said God, 'there's two of us. How much is it?' He dug around in his robes as if they might contain pockets. 'You got any money?' he asked Grace after he'd tugged his robes for a suitable period.

'Some,' she admitted. She'd raided as much as she could from Uncle Ray's stash. She'd felt it was the least he could do for her.

'We have no use for money,' said the man, 'it requires a functioning economy to make it more than scrap metal and paper. Our little Queendom relies on more direct methods than that.'

Grace took a step back, reminded of the old man and his roasting cat.

'A table with us costs a moderate favour per head,' the man explained. 'To be decided at a later date but on the understanding that said favour will be nothing too onerous. A bit of washing up, perhaps some laundry, or a pleasant song played on the guitar.'

'I don't play the guitar,' said God, 'but if you've come for favours you're in the right place. I'm God, you see, and can grant you whatever you wish.'

'I'm sure you can,' the man agreed, arching his eyebrows, 'but I assure you it won't be anything too greedy.'

'And you just trust us?' asked Grace. 'What's to stop us running off and never paying what we owe?'

'Nothing,' the man shrugged, 'as long as you think you can run faster than the Queen's forces. Non-payment of debts is punishable by death, regardless of the size of the favour.'

'That's a bit much,' said Grace.

'It works,' said the waiter.

'It's positively biblical!' said God with a big grin. 'No complaints here, let us in pal and we'll happily discharge our debts as and when the time comes.'

The man led them to their car, and gestured for them to sit.

'How is this going to work?' Grace asked, staring at the retrofitted carriage. Someone had torn out the bench seats and replaced them with a dining table. The two chairs and table were securely bolted in place and a harness hung from the back of each chair. The man lifted the harness and tapped the chair, instructing Grace to sit down. She did so and he strapped her in before moving to the other side of the table to do the same for God.

'The Cyclone is the latest in extreme dining, madame,' he explained, lighting a candle in the middle of the table. 'For the Coney Island visitor that simply doesn't have time to experience the ride *and* partake in lunch. Are either of you vegetarian?'

'I am,' Grace replied, thinking momentarily of the remains of her uncle.

He walked over to a cupboard set next to the ride controls, opened it and brought out two covered dinner plates. He placed them in front of Grace and God, lifting the dish to reveal their meals. Grace had an omelette with fries and salad, God had a steak. Both appeared to be hot, steaming on their wooden plates.

'As you are new to dining here at the Cyclone, allow me to offer you our novice service, free of charge.' He went back to the cupboard, returning with a gleaming silver hammer and a handful of nails. With great ceremony, he nailed the steak and omelette to the plates. 'I'm afraid that, with regards the sides, you're on your own, there are simply not enough hours in the day to allow me to nail each and every French fry, I suggest you keep your hand on them when approaching any fierce corners. Your drinks,' he tapped the pair of steel canisters fixed to the table, 'are best taken through a straw.'

He fed a thin length of plastic tubing into the top of each sealed cup and offered them the other end. 'Some customers tuck the tube behind their ear when chewing.'

'This is crazy,' laughed Grace.

'My darling girl,' the man said, smiling in the sort of way a serial killer might when you've just expressed an interest in dying, 'what isn't these days?'

With that he stepped back and threw the switch that set the car moving.

God shrugged and immediately set to shovelling the fries in his mouth. 'Better get these down quick,' he suggested. 'The steak can look after itself.'

Grace looked over his shoulder at the approaching incline and decided she may as well go with it. It had been a long time since anyone had cooked her a hot meal, she would have preferred to have been able to appreciate it in more relaxed circumstances but she wasn't going to waste the opportunity.

Like God, she went for the fries first, ignoring the cutlery as the car switched to a steep angle, mounting the incline in the tracks. She cupped her hands around the plate as all the food spilled towards her, pinching the fries in her fingers and shoving them in her mouth. Slowly, with the ratcheting of pulleys, the car crept towards the high point of the ride.

If she could only get the fries and salad done before they hit the top! The car flattened out at the crest of the incline, Grace still with a mouthful of salad and fried potato. God, his back to the ride, had a concerned look on his face. 'I know what's coming,' he said, his voice shaking, 'I know exactly what's coming.'

'You'll be fine,' she told him, 'just watch out for flying French fries.'

The car dropped, the candle blew out and God roared in shocked panic as his face filled with leaves of rocket and slices of onion. 'I don't like it!' he screamed.

Grace laughed and realised it was probably the first time she'd done so in longer than she could remember. She took a sip of her drink, diet soda, and pointed at God's steak. 'Get eating, my Lord,' she said, 'it'll get cold real quick at this speed.'

His cutlery was still in his hand and, to give him credit, he tried to cut the meat even as the car levelled out, rising again slightly and shifting into a tight bend. He had a forkful hovering at his lips when the car approached the next drop.

'Careful,' she shouted, not wanting to see him choke to death.

The car dropped again, shorter this time, before rising briefly.

'Now!' she shouted, putting a forkful of the omelette into her mouth as he did the same with his steak. 'Chew quickly.'

He did as she suggested, following her directions as she warned him of each dip and bend.

They rocked in their harnesses, doing their best to finish the food in front of them. As they finally drew level at the end of the ride, God was looking decidedly unwell.

'God didn't like his steak,' he announced, 'and would very much like to...' He unclipped his harness and ran down the steps to ground level where he darted behind the ride and began to be sick.

'Would sir like me to hold his beard for him while he takes care of business?' the waiter asked, smiling in pleasure at his customer's discomfort.

'He'll be fine,' said Grace. 'Is there a gratuity included?'

'I'm watching it right now,' the waiter said, chuckling at the sight of the vomiting God. Then he straightened his tie, gave a small bow and returned to where the next couple were waiting to be seated.

# Chapter Nine

IT TOOK GOD a short while to get over his disastrous lunch. Grace walked him down towards the beach, thinking the fresh air would help.

They sat and looked out on the ocean for half an hour or so. God went over to the water's edge to dip his beard in the surf and give it a clean, Grace watching him surrounded by inquisitive gulls. He refused to do the easy thing of just taking it off so was forced to bend down in the water, pressing his face against the incoming waves. By the time he returned he was looking very wet and distinctly sorry for himself.

'Sorry,' she said, 'I shouldn't have laughed. It wasn't a very nice lunch was it?'

'It's fine,' he replied, trying to make light of it. 'I could have risen above it but I thought it might be instructive to experience it just as a mortal would. It's easy to become isolated when you're a deity, immune to the human condition. I find it rewarding to remind myself from time to time what it is to live like one of you.'

'It keeps you grounded,' she said, doing her best to sound sincere.

'Precisely,' he agreed.

'When I was a kid,' she said, 'I used to go to church sometimes. Not with Uncle Ray, he never had time for that sort of thing, but Auntie Lois would come over and take me to to the First Pentecostal. It freaked me out to begin with, all those people shouting, screaming and flinging themselves to the floor. It was so loud. It seemed, I don't know, *needy*. Like the people were desperate to prove themselves in front of one another rather than to a God.' She corrected herself. 'You, that is. You know, it seemed as if it was all about who could shout the loudest, who was the most overcome, who was the most blessed. I just used to sit there while Aunt Lois threw herself around and people spoke in tongues. I know it was supposed to be a good thing but it took a few weeks before I stopped finding it terrifying.'

'Those happy clappers,' he said, 'they're a funny bunch. You don't need to shout, people, I'm right here. Still, whatever floats your holy boat I guess. I'm not judgemental. Well, I am sometimes, comes with the position, but, you know, generally speaking I try not to take sides. Humans are weird, they always think they know best. Like little kids at a party, showing off and trying to get your attention all the time. Some of 'em float around being all serious, acting as if butter wouldn't melt in their mouths. Some are loud and abrasive. Others flip around or slide along the floor on their knees, trying to impress with athleticism. At the end of the day they're all the same, just wanting daddy to give them a little love.'

In front of them, the sea crashed onto the beach, in the distance clouds rolled by without a care in the world.

'You know,' said Grace. 'I feel weird. I'm actually relaxed. I really shouldn't be should I? Not here, where we don't know what's going on and what we're going to do. But after weeks of being on my own it's just, yeah, nice to be sat next to someone.'

'Someone who doesn't want to kill you.'

'Precisely. I think I'd sort of given up on that.'

'In truth,' he said, 'I hadn't wanted to come here. You know that. I was comfortable in my life at the church.'

'Beating up cars.'

'Beating up cars,' he agreed. 'But it's no bad thing to be spontaneous. To get out of your daily routine and remind yourself why it is you created a world in the first place. I'd prefer it if it wasn't so broken, I'll admit, but that's still one hell of a view.'

She nodded and took his arm. 'You did good with the beaches, don't let anyone ever tell you otherwise.'

# Chapter Ten

THEY RETURNED TO the ticket booth outside the Queen's castle. Both were licking at ice creams they'd bought from a street vendor who wanted no more payment than someone to scratch that part of your back you never could quite reach yourself.

'That's the business,' he'd sighed as God had worked him over with his nails, 'Goddamn that's good.'

God had raised his eyebrows at that but said nothing, not wishing to jeopardise the soft scoop of pistachio he had his holy eyes on.

A small line of eight or nine people had formed at the booth.

'Two to see the Queen,' said Grace to the albino girls still manning the booth. 'How much?'

'No charge,' the girl said, 'though once you have a ticket you have to go in. If you have to go in you have to see Her

Majesty. If you have to see Her Majesty you have to have a reason. Understand?'

'Well, we wouldn't be here if we didn't have a reason,' Grace replied.

'Your call,' the girl said, tearing off two numbered tickets and handing them to Grace. 'You're nine and ten, each session has a two minute window so you won't have too long to wait.'

Grace gave God his ticket and they joined the end of the line behind a thin woman who towered above them, her arms and legs unnaturally elongated.

'What are you here for?' the woman asked.

'I want permission to visit my brother,' Grace explained. 'You?'

'I need to move from my place on 21st, ceilings are too damned low. My back's killing me. I know a guy with a loft on 15th that's willing to trade but I need Her Majesty's blessing.'

'Good luck.'

'It's no big deal,' the woman said, ducking involuntarily as a gull swooped past, 'as long as she's not in one of her moods.'

'Have you met her before then?' asked God.

'Oh yeah, loads of times. She's great normally but, you know, on her bad days she can be a bit hard to please. I heard from Kookie at the Surf Shack, you know, the coffee place on the boardwalk...?'

Grace and God shook their heads. 'We only just got here,' Grace explained.

'You should go, he does great shrimp latte. Anyway, he tells me she's still pissed 'cos of the thing with the squids.'

'Squids?'

'You know? With the balloons?'

Grace and God shook their heads again.

'Right,' the woman nodded, 'only just got here. There was a thing with some squids. And balloons. Caused a lot of fuss. Anyway, so Kookie says she's still in a rough mood over it and he told me to wait until things had calmed down but, you know? I can only take so much of those damn ceilings. My scalp's covered in scabs and white paint, know what I'm saying? I need out of there, like yesterday.'

'I'm sure you'll be fine,' said Grace, 'as you say, it's no big deal.' She looked at God. 'I just hope we can say the same.'

At two o'clock sharp, a pair of guards appeared at the entrance to the castle. They were dressed in a rough clash between gaudy clown's outfits and chainmail. Their faces were painted black but with a clear section around their eyes and mouth, an approximation of knights' visors done with makeup.

'OK,' said one of them, 'who's up first?'

A man with scaly skin held up his hand and offered his ticket.

'Right,' said the guard, 'walk this way pal.'

They led him inside and the line shuffled one step closer to the door.

After a short wait there was a sound of screaming. The door opened and the lizard-like man was ejected, flung by the two guards, landing in a furious heap at Grace's feet.

'You're barred for two months,' said the guard, 'and next time keep your tongue to yourself.'

'I can't help it!' the lizard man shouted, his long tongue whipping out and wrapping itself around Grace's ankle.

He tried to speak again but the noise was unintelligible as he fought to retract his tongue.

Grace, wincing, bent down and tried to help but he slapped her hands away.

'Bad enough I gotta taste your jeans, girl,' he said once free, holding a hand in front of his mouth to try to control the errant tongue. 'I don't want to taste whatever you've been touching too.'

He turned back to the guards. 'Come on guys, do a man a solid would you?'

The guard shrugged. 'You slap your tongue around a Queen's face she's going to lose her cool, what did you expect?'

'Speciesist!' the man shouted and, once again, his tongue lashed out, this time wrapping around his own wrist. 'Ah fa fags sak,' he grunted, wandering off in defeat, slowly uncurling the tongue with his free hand.

'This ain't a good start,' said the tall woman. 'Why did I have to pick today?'

Grace was thinking much the same thing as the guard led the next visitor in.

# Chapter Eleven

FINALLY, THE TALL woman having been led in by the guards, Grace and God were next in line.

'I think the best way is deference,' said God. 'Queens aren't like Gods, they like a lot of bowing.'

'I thought Gods liked that too?'

'Well, averting your eyes from someone's ineffable coolness is one thing—we'd have a lot less dead people in the world if people didn't want to look the celestial smack bang in the eyes—but, speaking personally, I find excess praise wearing. My ego isn't so fractured that I need everyone telling me how wonderful I am all the time. I created a whole universe, you really think I need someone else to tell me I'm amazing?'

The door opened and the guards reappeared.

'Did she get her new apartment?' Grace asked.

One of the guards shrugged. 'To be honest I wasn't

listening, you tune out after a while. She hasn't been beheaded or anything so odds are she got what she wanted.'

'Beheaded?' Grace asked as the guards led them both in. 'Is that an option?'

'Who knows? It all depends on her hangover.'

Beyond the door was a bright, plastic corridor filled with the roar of the pumps that kept the castle upright. It was extremely difficult to walk, all four of them bouncing from one wall to the other as they tried to move forward.

'Do you get used to this?' Grace asked as she fell at the feet of one of the guards.

'Used to what?' he replied, bouncing on the spot.

The corridor veered to the right and they found themselves in the throne room. Fake, plastic sconces flickered with battery-powered bulbs; incense burned, a layer of pungent smoke hovering beneath the plastic ceiling and, in the corner, a tatty turntable played medieval music, the needle skipping every time someone tried to move.

The Queen was sat in a reclining leather chair, a large soda wedged into a cup holder in the arm. She looked to be in her early sixties but it was hard to tell as she'd clearly spent a good deal of her life living in doorways. Her hair was matted and wild, great horns of it, grey and white, stabbing upwards from her blotchy scalp. Somewhere in all of it, she'd managed to lodge a cardboard crown, the fast-food chain logo on it scribbled out in pen with QUEEN written over it in big capitals. Her face was wrinkled in the sort of way a bottom might be if you left it in a bath for a few weeks. She was poking at one of her remaining teeth with a fat finger, a mole on her upper lip writhing as if trying to find somewhere less awkward to be.

She was wearing a bright, satin frock but the effect was spoiled by the stained overcoat she wore over it, its pockets bulging, its lapels curled like winter leaves. Woollen, fingerless gloves poked out of the sleeves, one pink and one green, both smudged black at the palms.

She was, quite simply, the grottiest looking Queen Grace could imagine.

At her side, cleaning his fingernails with a knife better suited to gutting large wildlife, was an equally rough looking man. He was wearing a leather jacket several sizes too large and a Spider-Man T-shirt several sizes too small. His lower-half was almost covered by tatty long-johns, his knees poking out to grab some fresh air.

'Say hi to the Queen, dudes,' he announced, not looking up.

'Hi, Your Majesty,' Grace said, bowing as low as she could without losing her balance on the unreliable floor. She noticed God wasn't bowing so she kicked him in the shin.

'I'm God,' he said, 'wouldn't it be weird to bow?'

'You said it was important!'

'I meant for you, I don't want to give her ideas above her station.'

'Just do it! Please!'

'Fine,' he gave a brief bow. 'Pleased to make your acquaintance, Your Majesty,' he said. 'Please don't let the bowing deity thing go to your head.'

The Queen looked over to her aide. 'Either he's been drinking or I started again and didn't notice. Did I start drinking again?'

'No Your Majesty, I think it must be him.'

'Please don't be frightened,' said God. 'I am here as a benevolent God, accompanying my friend Grace. It's her that seeks your help.'

'You're God?' the Queen asked, chuckling in a manner that agitated years of accumulated phlegm.

'The one and only, but as I say, this isn't an official visit. You're not dead or anything, I'm just here as a plus one.' He took a step back, gesturing for Grace to move forward.

'Hang fire, guy,' said the aide, 'you get a ticket?'

'Absolutely,' God replied, holding it up, 'all official.'

'Then you have to ask for something. That's how it works.'

'I have a request,' said Grace, trying to bring things back on track.

'Babe, I don't doubt it, but the dude needs one too. You get a ticket you make a request, quid pro and status quo, you know?'

God rocked from side to side on the inflatable floor. 'I really don't want anything. I'm God, not wanting anything is part of the deal.'

'Then you're in contempt of the Queen's court and must pay, like, a forfeit.'

'Maybe I can think of something in that case...' God scratched at his false beard. 'My sandals are getting a bit tatty.'

'Bro'! You can't just make stuff up on the spot! You broke the rules, suck it up.'

'Let the girl speak,' said the Queen, spitting into her soda cup, 'then we'll decide what to do with both of 'em.'

Grace rubbed at her face in frustration. This was not going well.

'I ask for passage to Rikers Island,' she said. 'You can't get there by land at the moment...'

'Damn right you can't,' said the Queen. 'You seen what's happened to Queens?' She looked at her aide. 'I hate that name, Corman, can't we have it changed. I mean... it ain't mine is it?'

'You wouldn't want it,' Corman replied. He looked at Grace. 'You know what the average lifespan is of people that enter Queens these days?' She shook her head. 'Eight minutes. Freakazoid, baby, they're dropping like, you know, flies over there.'

'Why do you want to go to Rikers, anyway?' asked the Queen. 'You done something wrong?'

'My brother's there.'

'Since when? Before The Change?'

'Yes.'

'Then he's probably long gone. He's likely dead, girl, you know that, yes?'

'He's the only family I have left. If you were me wouldn't you try?'

The Queen laughed. 'Kid, if my family were still alive, I'd be hunting them down with a crossbow right now. Blood don't mean a thing. You make your own family in this world, you choose them and stick by them.'

'I choose to stick by him.'

The Queen shrugged. 'It's a big ask, you know that? I mean, you want a boat and a free pass all the way up the river. That ain't something I just give away.'

'I'm willing to do whatever needs to be done,' Grace stood as proud as possible given how much the room was moving.

The Queen looked at Corman. 'We fed the babies this week?'

Corman's face fell. 'Really? You're going to ask her to do that?'

'It needs doing and nobody else is stepping up to the plate.'

'Whatever it is,' said Grace, 'I'll do it. No question.'

Corman shook his head. 'Kid, you ain't going to last long in this world with an attitude like that.'

'You will enter Dreamland,' said the Queen, 'and you will feed the babies.'

'Dreamland?'

'Dreamland was one of the first amusement parks on Coney Island,' said Corman, 'since The Change did its thing it's back. And weirder than ever.'

'OK,' Grace nodded. 'What babies?'

'You don't know about the babies?' the Queen asked. 'Years ago, one of Dreamland's exhibits was a room of babies in incubators. Back then they weren't medically approved. So people brought their kids to the guy. Doctor... erm... whatever... don't really matter... and they put them in these things. He saved a lot of kids' lives.'

'And made a lot of dough,' added Corman.

'But they're hungry,' said the Queen, 'and they're causing problems.'

'Surely,' said God, stepping forward, 'if they're in incubators then they don't need food, aren't they on tubes and stuff?'

'You'll see for yourself,' said the Queen. 'They've got a bit out of control. We should have them put down really but, well, they're only babies. Sort of. In a way. Anyway. That's the deal, take it or leave it.'

'I take it.'

Corman sighed. 'Poor kid,' he said, 'that's harsh man.'

'I'm Queen!' she shouted. 'And what I say goes. If you have a problem with that you can go with her.'

'Surely if it's that dangerous it's not really fair to send her,' said God.

'I can manage, thank you,' said Grace. She knew he meant well but she wished he'd stop suggesting she was incapable.

'But now you open your mouth, "God,"' said the Queen, 'we still need to decide what to do with you, don't we? You broke the rules and now you're trying to tell me my job. That sort of thing doesn't go down well in The Queendom of Coney Island, boy, whoever you are. Your punishment will be severe. It will be savage. It will forever be spoken of in legend as a thing to give children nightmares. It will, in fact, probably be the death of you.'

'I can't be killed...' God started to say but Grace interrupted him.

'What are you going to do to him?' she asked.

'What do you think, kid?' The Queen laughed. 'He gets to go with you!'

# Chapter Twelve

Dreamland opened its doors in 1904, the result of three and half million dollars—a staggering sum in those days—and a desire on the part of its owner, William H. Reynolds, to outdo the neighbouring attractions of Luna Park. It closed seven years later after a fire destroyed the majority of it. The fire was caused by an upturned bucket of pitch igniting the Hell Gate ride. The infernal irony was thicker than the insurance pay out and Dreamland dreamed no more.

In those intervening seven years it had seen zoos, freaks shows, thrill rides, dancing and drama. It was the very epitome of the American Dream, beautiful, aspirational, grotesque and ambitious.

Post-Change it had reoccupied its previous location off Surf Avenue, a fluctuating dream of a dream. A fifteen acre plot built on the fantasies and fears of every visitor who had ever danced in the ballroom, splashed in the lagoon or gazed in unashamed wonder at the diminutive residents of the Lilliputian village known as Midget City. It was the ultimate expression of how The Change had brought the architecture of the world to life, brought flesh to thoughts, horror to the mundane.

And Grace and God were going to go inside.

'Dreamland?' asked the owner of the Cyclone, a man they now knew as Ken Dante, onetime short-order chef and occasional petty crook. 'Nobody with an ounce of sense would set foot in there.'

'So everyone keeps telling me,' Grace replied, washing another plate and handing it to God to dry.

'You'll both be dead before the day's out,' Dante clarified, should they have been unsure as to his opinion on the place. 'No doubt about it.'

'And we're spending our last night on earth washing up your dishes,' she said.

'A debt's a debt,' he replied, 'but I appreciate it. If you'd decided to leave it until after your mission for the Queen I'd likely have been down on the deal.'

'I could just wave my hand,' said God, 'and they would all be clean. But sometimes...'

'It's good to experience things as mortals do,' finished Grace.

'Precisely,' he agreed. 'It gives me an excellent sense of perspective.'

'He's mad,' Dante whispered to Grace, 'you do know that don't you?'

'Who cares?' she replied. 'Do you know somewhere we might be able to sleep for the night? Apparently it's even more dangerous if we go into Dreamland at night so we're supposed to wait until first thing tomorrow.'

'I can probably hook you up, it'll cost you...' He stopped himself. 'What's the point? You'll never be able to repay me. I'll look on it as an act of charity.'

'You're too kind.'

'Hell, once we're done I'll even throw in a night out. The condemned deserve a good farewell.'

'What sort of night out?' God asked. 'I mean, I'm pretty open-minded, whatever some people think, but still, I have to watch my reputation. God can't be seen living it up in a strip-joint.'

'Nothing wrong with a creator admiring his creation,' said Dante, 'but nah... there's a party going on over at Edina's, I was going to look in anyway so I may as well take you two along.'

# Chapter Thirteen

EDINA'S WAS A raucous shack of neon and corrugated iron that had been constructed on the boardwalk. It threw its light and noise out towards the crashing ocean as if trying to lure unwary sailors. If any landed they would, at least, be assured a good time. The music was just shy of an act of warfare. The band attacked their instruments as if fighting for their lives; the resultant sound managed to be both euphoric and terrifying. The large crowd pogoing on the rudimentary dance floor frequently dived for cover as a wave of bass poleaxed the unwary.

The bar fizzed like a stick of dynamite. Bottles often as smashed as those trying to get their lips around them.

It was the sort of bar that reminded you of nature: potentially fatal chaos somehow holding itself together despite the lack of observable controlling factors.

Edina was six foot of muscles and weird bone structure,

a weight lifter whose body twitched and flexed as if her taut skin were filled with piglets wired up to the mains. Every now and then she would lift up tables and seated clientele. The impromptu weights would invariably keep drinking even as their scalps touched the thatched roof. Clearly a degree of vertical shift was just something you accepted if you wanted to drink at Edina's.

God was keeping his distance, sipping a glass of wine and watching as Grace jumped up and down on the dance floor. Dante had danced with her for a while then moved off to help himself to some of the barbecue that was hissing, smoking (and in some cases writhing) on a long griddle just along the boardwalk.

God made a great deal about wanting to understand the human condition but, of course, he wasn't quite as naive as he pretended to be. He saw the stern, focused look on Grace's face as she danced. He saw the ferocious energy she was trying to work off. Every move was an act of violence rather than joy. She was sweating, teeth clenched, feet stamping; it was fury with added rhythm. Grace was, unsurprisingly, a very screwed-up kid. She tried to hide it but here, when the beat was upon her, it showed clearly.

It was, or so it seemed to him, part of a God's duty to help his children. Policies of non-intervention aside, he decided it was important that he tried to improve her lot. Restoring the world might be an ecclesiastical transgression too far but saving the soul of one good kid?

That was far game, he decided. He'd stick with her and do the best for her he could.


GRACE TOOK A break from dancing at around midnight. Her legs and arms ached and she just wanted to find some air.

She looked around for God but couldn't see him in the crowd. Deciding she'd stumble upon him sooner or later, she headed outside onto the beach, walking towards the sea.

All around her, breakaway groups from the party had set up on the sand. Small bonfires flickered in the night, casting shadows of people laughing and loving their way through the dark hours.

She walked a little further up the beach, wanting to find her own place. She sat down in the sand at the edge of the water and stared out at the mirrored night on the ocean.

The calm she had always known—that numb, distant dislocation from the world that had allowed her to survive both before and after The Change—had been shaken up. She felt bursts of anger, fear and agitation all churning away inside her. She took deep breaths, listening to the sound of the waves. She tried to force away the pounding of the music from the bar, the sound of the other people. She imagined herself back in the darkness of the cabin, cocooned against the world. Rocking back and forth on the soft sand she visualised swallowing every strong emotion inside her, pressing them down and down until they were lost inside; muffled, dead.

She breathed out, calm and cold, empty again.

'Hey kid, you cool?'

She looked up to see Corman, the Queen's aide. He was draining a bottle of beer in his left hand so he could get started on the one in his right.

'Cool?' she asked. 'Should I be, given what I'm supposed to face tomorrow?'

He nodded, staring at the empty bottle of beer as if it might contain some important answers. Finally, deciding that, like most of us, it contained nothing but stale air, he lobbed it into the ocean and took a sip from its full replacement. 'She was kind of full on,' he said. 'You never can tell with her. Sometimes she's soft, kind, do anything for anyone. Other times she's... well, she's kind of mean, you know?'

'And today was a mean day.'

'You got it, kid. But you never know, you might be ok. Least there's two of you. You can watch each other's backs.'

'As some freak sticks something sharp in them?'

He shrugged. 'I wish I could help ya, kid. It sucks the big one. Truth be told she don't know what to do with the place, you know? It's here in her patch but she can't control it, not like everywhere else. What are the things inside? The original inhabitants? Ghosts? Some kind of freaky mixture of the two?' He took another mouthful of beer. 'Give it to you straight, it's something she just can't get that mind of hers around. So she pushes it off onto someone else until she can think of a way of dealing with it. Tomorrow that's you and your guy with the beard.'

'And the day after?'

'Way she's been behaving who knows? This is all new you know? We're still finding our feet really. Right now she's the Queen Bee, 'cos she may not look like much but she's got it where it counts. She built most of this place out of this,' he tapped his head, 'it's like she's its heart somehow. The thing that makes it all tick. I guess she lived here so long, years of sleeping on these streets that she's linked to it. They're joined.' He sighed. 'She was sick for a couple of days and the whole of West 18th was shaking. It's like they're one and the same thing. I don't know, I can't get my head around it, who the hell can?

'But the thing with Dreamland, that ain't part of her. That's something she never knew. As much as things have changed, distorted, got whacked, it's still, at heart, Coney Island. Dreamland is before her time. She ain't in touch with it. That freaks her out. I think she'd be happier if the whole place burned down.'

'And you'd let her do that?'

'All I know is that she has power here and, most days, that power's good. There's places in this city where a man can die just by sticking his head out the window but here, life's pretty good, and a lot of that's to do with her. A few months, that's all and we have ourselves a community, we have a home that works, where you can just chill and know you'll probably wake up in the morning.'

'She's not just a mad woman, I get it. Doesn't help me and God much.'

'Where did you find that dude? I mean, I know the world's hinky as hell these days but you've gotten yourself a real whacko there.'

'I like him.'

'Fair enough.'

Grace looked up to see God walking towards them, his robes ruffling in the breeze. As he walked past a small group, gathered around one of the bonfires, they gave him a whooping cheer. It was mocking, of course, but if he knew that he didn't let it show. He stopped, raised his hands and uttered some form of benediction that was lost in the wind. Then he turned back to her and kept walking.

'There you are,' he said, 'just as I thought. I think it's time we retired for the night. Not that I need sleep of course, but you at least should be refreshed for the morning, we have a trial ahead of us.'

Grace nodded.

'Dante's spoken to someone at Edina's,' he continued, 'apparently there's space at a place just around the corner. Someone owed him I guess and putting us up for the night clears the debt.'

'Let's go then,' she said, turning to look at Corman one last time. 'Maybe I'll see you tomorrow.'

'Maybe you will kid,' he said, raising his beer towards her. 'Here's hoping!'

# Chapter Fourteen

GRACE HAD HALF-expected there would be some sort of fuss to usher them in, maybe an appearance from the Queen herself, a proclamation of their aims, a brief ceremony to get them over the threshold. In actuality there was just one of the guards, sat on the sidewalk with a clipboard. Next to him was a large, knotted sack.

'Just to confirm your agreement,' he said, not getting up, just handing the clipboard over. 'You go in there, feed the babies and, should you return—which you probably won't—the Queen of Coney Island guarantees that she will supply you with transport and authority to travel up the river as far as Rikers.'

'Right,' said Grace, staring at the hastily scribbled contract. 'And I'm supposed to sign this am I?'

'Yeah,' said the guard, staring over the road towards a woman who was opening her tattooing parlour. Grace couldn't swear whether it was the woman or the notion of a tattoo that had him looking dreamy but she had a fair idea.

'You got a pen?' she asked.

'Nah,' he replied.

'Then I can't sign it.'

'Whatever,' he took it back from her, continuing to watch the woman across the road as she unwound the awning above her store window. 'Food's in the sack.'

'Paperwork is the creation of the devil,' God said, 'we're better off without it.'

'We'll sign it when we get back,' she said.

'Absolutely,' he agreed, hoisting the sack onto his shoulder, 'give us half an hour and we'll be demanding a boat. I'm God, I know this for a fact. Probably.'

The entrance to Dreamland was dominated by a towering edifice of white stone inset with hundreds of old electric bulbs. Even in the brightness of day those bulbs glowed with a liquid light that looked as if it might burn should it pour on you.

Bostock – The Animal King invited you to sample his zoological marvels. "Continuous lions, tigers, bears, panthers, wolves, elephants and hyenas" were promised according to the signs that stood either side of the ticket booth. On the wall a painting of Frank Bostock, a veritable vision of relaxed British tweed. The sort of moustache that had once conquered nations jutted either side of his lips.

For a fleeting moment, the ethereal ghost of a baby elephant pushed between them, its trunk curled skywards as it ran towards the road, then it was gone.

To the right of Bostock's Animal Arena stood the main entrance to Dreamland. Entering, the park opened out before them. At the centre was the White Tower, rising up over a hundred metres into the sky, its Spanish-styled peak was said to offer a view of forty miles in each direction. Bristling with lights it pulsed at the heart of the midway, a beacon of ostentation writ large over the entire park. To the rear of it was the lagoon, surrounded by the tight loop of the racetrack. All around this central feature ran the rides and exhibition halls. Everything from the Canals of Venice gondola ride to the Midget City exhibition and the Fighting the Flames fire-fighting display. Spectators gathered in the giant amphitheatre to witness the blazing spectacle that employed a grand total of 2,000 performers.

At the far end of the park, where the midway met the pier and the ocean beyond, the duel chutes of the flume ride lifted into the sky. To their left was the Leap Frog railway where two trains took it in turns to travel over one another, traversing the tracks built into the roof of each carriage.

To the far right, built onto the pier was the giant ballroom, 25,000 square feet of dance floor hopping to the sound of the band.

Dreamland certainly fought hard to live up to its name.

'It's amazing...' Grace sighed. 'I've never seen anywhere like it.'

God shrugged. 'Not bad I suppose. Pretty impressive, you know, for humans.'

'It's going to take us all day just to find the babies let alone feed them.'

God pointed to their immediate right where a sign announced Infant Incubators with Living Infants. 'There you go.'

'No way,' Grace walked up to the door of the building where another sign cheerfully announced All the World Loves a Baby. 'This is crazy,' she said. 'Who puts baby incubators in a theme park anyway?'

'It's like the Queen told us,' said God, joining her, 'even though the technology for baby incubators existed at the beginning of the twentieth century they weren't adopted by hospitals. For a start, nobody could afford them. Then this guy has a bright idea of using them as exhibits. He opened "child hatcheries" all over the place. Saved lots of premature babies, made a lot of money.'

'Guess that's kind of cool.'

'You bet, try the door.'

Grace opened it and they stepped inside where they were faced with an empty ticket booth and, beyond that, a long corridor alongside a glass partition. Beyond the partition was a room set up like a hospital, bright white with rows of incubators and medical cabinets.

'Can you see any babies?' Grace asked. 'They look empty.' She pressed herself up against the glass and peered through. 'Definitely empty, in fact most of them look smashed...' She moved to the door at the far end of the corridor, it wasn't locked. She looked at God, who shrugged.

Grace opened the door and immediately fell backwards as it was slammed hard against her by something on the other side. Flat on the floor she looked up to see a gang of babies flooding out of the door. They moved at great speed, their chubby arms and legs slapping against the ground as they made a break for freedom.

She gave a short cry as they poured over her, moving like a wave of fat, pink beetles. In a matter of seconds they'd darted past God and on towards the still open door leading out onto the midway.

'Shut the door!' Grace shouted but there was no way God could keep up with the speedy infants as they crawled out to freedom.

'Right,' said God, 'that's probably not good, is it?'

# Chapter Fifteen

SOME DISTANCE AWAY, beyond the air ships ride and the Fighting the Flames amphitheatre sat the Japanese Tea Rooms. It had been considerable decades since it had seen a paying customer but, since it had been dragged back into existence, there was one man who made considerable use of its facilities.

He sat at the centre table, leather gauntlets draped over the back of the chair next to him. He always wore the gauntlets in public, it stopped people staring at the wooden stump that had replaced his left hand. On the table was an immaculately arranged set of crockery. A cup, a teapot, a jug of hot water and a small container of green tea. The man's hand moved from one to the next, enjoying the ritual of preparing his drink as much—perhaps even more than—the drink itself. He added tea to the pot, poured in the water and waited, occasionally nudging the crockery tiny distances away from each other so it was even more perfectly arranged. After four minutes had elapsed, he lifted the pot and poured himself a small cup of the tea.

'Gerry,' said a woman's voice, light suddenly flooding the room, 'I think someone just released the babies.'

The cup hovered just below Colonel Gerry Ballard's lips, a long sigh blowing tiny waves across its hot surface.

'Gloria,' he said, 'what sort of idiot would do a thing like that?'

He looked up towards the flickering creature that had been the love of his life. Now neither of them was quite alive anymore but their bond remained firm. A shimmering presence of projected light and crinkling celluloid, the cinematic spectre of a movie star gone by. When she moved the air crackled, the sepia-toned beauty of her face flipping between static poses, from innocent to sultry, comedic to terrified. Old Hollywood stars never really died, they lived on in light and plastic.

'They came from outside,' said Gloria, adopting a pose that she felt best suited explanations, her finger on her chin, her eyes gazing upwards in thought, 'sent by the Queen.'

'That meddlesome tramp.' He took a sip of his tea, damned if he was going to have the moment entirely ruined. With a careful finger, he smoothed his waxed moustache, its tips tapering to curls either side of his face. 'Does she not realise what happens whenever she sends people here? To hell with the babies, if there are visitors we've worse problems to contend with. I suppose I shall have to sort it out as always.'

'My handsome soldier,' said Gloria, her pose turning to one of lust, big eyes and pouting lips. 'How I long to touch you.'

He leaned close and kissed the air an inch or so away from her face, wincing slightly from the heat she gave off. 'If I must burn, my darling,' he said. 'I'll burn with you.'

# Chapter Sixteen

THE NEWS HAD also spread to Midget City. The three hundred residents of the diminutive village were happily minding their own business, getting irate at the twee, patronising and frankly offensive fixtures and fittings of their little town when an announcement came over the tannoy.

'Intruder alert,' it announced, 'punters on the midway. They've set the babies free and God knows how long we have before Dreamland wakes. Duty guards should report to the front gate with their tools. Now.'

Baron Fabrizzi, who had spent the last ten minutes contentedly trying to select a silk handkerchief for his breast pocket, plucked the scarlet with yellow polka dots from its hanger and slipped it into place. Stopping only to add an extra sheen to his patent leather shoes, he made his way to the front gate as quickly as he could be bothered.

'What the hell kept you Fabrizzi?' asked the duty guard leader, a bitter man by the name of Horlicks. 'This is an emergency.'

'All the more reason to face it with élan,' Fabrizzi replied, winking at Lucy O'Neil, a young lady he had taken a shine to over the last couple of days (partly, but not entirely, because all the other ladies he'd taken a shine to recently were no longer talking to him). Lucy rolled her eyes but he was pretty sure he glimpsed a momentary smile on her lips. That was enough, he decided, that was something to work on.

At any given time on the roster, thirty of the residents were on duty as the guard. They were gathered now, irritated that something genuinely annoying had occurred on their watch, except for Horlicks. Horlicks loved a bit of drama.

'We need to get out there!' he shouted, several members of the guard taking a step back because he was so loud. 'Deal with the punters and round the little snots up. Collect a net and stick and let's get this done in double-quick time.'

One by one they picked up their tools, Fabrizzi doing his best to stay close to Lucy.

'Let's do this!' Horlicks screamed with such enthusiasm that a number of people were heard to comment on the likelihood of his bursting something.

# Chapter Seventeen

THE WORD ALSO spread to the Circus Sideshow where it was met with less enthusiasm.

'That's all we need,' complained Jolly Irene as she slowly shifted her three hundred odd kilos from one chair to another. Neither chair received her without complaint. 'Now everyone will be worked up and they'll take it out on us.'

'As always,' Toney the Alligator Boy agreed, scratching at his scaled skin.

'Of course,' said Jean Libbera, otherwise known as the Double-Bodied Man thanks to the extra torso that dangled from his midriff, 'if we were to send out a small party to help, we might get some of the credit. Maybe even a bit of respect for once.' The extra torso clapped its spindly hands in appreciation of his fine idea.

'Well,' said Jolly Irene, 'you can count me out. I'm pooped just thinking about it.'

'Well,' said Toney, 'there's always the kids.'

'Yeah,' agreed Jean, 'this is work for the young. Teach 'em a bit of responsibility. 'Bout time they pulled their weight around here.'

They turned to look towards the two small figures that, until now, had been doing their best to avoid attention.

'Really?' said one. 'You're going to make this our problem?'

'Typical,' said the other, 'they pick on you and then you pick on us. One day we'll find someone *we* can pick on.'

Toney clipped him around the ear with a scaled hand. 'Stop complaining, you've never had it so good. Now get out there.'

# Chapter Eighteen

GRACE AND GOD were standing on the midway not really knowing what to do next.

'If we just leave...' Grace started to say.

'Then we won't have fulfilled our part of the contract,' said God, 'and the Queen will have our heads—well, your head at least—stuck on a spike at the top of her bouncy castle.'

'So we have to find them.'

'Yes.'

'Even though it could take us weeks.'

'Yes.'

'I'm beginning to wish I'd just risked Queens. Did you manage to count them?'

'I did!' God was pleased to be able to offer a positive answer. 'There were sixteen of them.'

'Brilliant.'

They made their way along the street, heading towards the ocean. Every now and then, out of the corner of their eyes, they would catch a glimpse of something moving but, by the time they'd turned to look there was nothing there.

'Hang on,' said Grace, 'what about the food? Maybe we can use that to lure them?'

'Good plan,' said God, dashing back to fetch the sack. While he was gone, Grace looked up at the airships ride, in reality wooden gondolas swinging at the end of steel cables. Despite the fact that nobody was on the ride, the gondolas kept spinning, whirling round and around, waiting for someone to join them.

As she watched she saw movement in one of the gondolas; one of the babies had somehow managed to climb up there and was now hopping up and down, its gurgling laughter just audible over the creak of the cables.

'Well, how are we supposed to get it down from there?' she wondered.

'What?' asked God, returning with the sack.

She pointed at the gleeful baby in the sky above them.

'Oh,' God adjusted his beard, 'that's a pain in the ass.'

'Let's see if we can draw its attention with some of the food,' suggested Grace, working at the knot in the sack. 'If it managed to get up there it must be able to get back down.'

Just as the knot came undone, the sack began writhing and, determined not to get caught out again, Grace cinched it tight, just as a bright red object flew out.

'The food's trying to escape too!' she shouted, fighting to retie the knot in the bag.

'I told you didn't I?' said God, staring at the object that had escaped the sack: it was an apple, two broad leaves jutting from its stalk fluttering like the wings of a bird. 'Never trust an apple.'

It hovered in front of them for a moment then flew up to where the baby had stopped bouncing up and down in the gondola and was watching the apple's approach, a greedy look in its eye. As the apple passed, it leapt from the gondola, grabbing the fruit in midair. For a moment it hung there, the apple beating its makeshift wings even faster as it fought to stay airborne. Slowly, it began to sink back towards the ground, unable to keep both itself and the baby afloat.

God chased after it as it descended, hoisting his robes so that he could run along the midway, eyes to the sky as it spiralled down.

The baby landed, rather gracefully, in a seated position, just next to the entrance to the hippodrome race track. The baby smiled, then opened its mouth, its jaw distending like that of a snake, and swallowed the apple whole.

Before it had a chance to move, God had grabbed it and bundled it inside his robes. 'I got one!' he shouted in triumph.

'Great,' said Grace, 'fifteen more to go.'

# Chapter Nineteen

'WHAT DO YOU plan to do, my love?' asked Gloria, hanging back from the light of outside, not wanting to lose any of her brilliance.

'The only thing I can do,' Colonel Gerry replied, loading his rifle, and pulling a spare bandolier of cartridges over his shoulder, 'shoot them. The babies too I think. Solve the problem once and for all. Put the damn things down. They're a menace. Vermin. They should be treated as such.'

'They're only babies darling,' said Gloria, adopting a shocked expression, 'if only we'd had our time I had hoped that one day we might have...'

'Babies? Pah! Do babies run that fast? Eat that way? They're disgusting, my little lotus petal, and they'll soon be floating face down in the Atlantic.'

He marched out into the daylight, his rifle firm in his

grasp. Behind him, hanging in the shadows where her ethereal body held its substance, Gloria watched him go.

# Chapter Twenty

GOD CAME JOGGING back from the incubator room having locked away their first captured baby.

'I don't know why they were all making such a fuss about this place,' he said. 'Weird it may be but it's hardly life-threatening is it?'

Grace had been thinking the same thing but, unlike God who seemed positively cheery about it all, she'd felt sure that the lack of lethal attacks could only mean that something awful was bound to happen soon.

'It all seems too quiet,' she said, looking up at the beacon tower, her hands resting on the wooden rail that surrounded the airships ride. 'I don't trust it.'

Suddenly, the handrail glowed beneath her hands and she snatched them back.

'Are you alright?' asked God.

Grace nodded. 'The handrail got hot.'

God touched it carefully. 'It does seem warm,' he admitted. 'It looks strange too.'

It wasn't glowing anymore but the paint appeared thicker, the colour sharper, an effect that was working its way along the whole rail. All sign of age was slowly vanishing as if the wood were renewing itself, becoming as flawless as it would have been on the day the park had first opened.

'It's…' She tried to think of the right word. 'Renewing?'

'Waking up,' said God, 'returning to life.'

'Is that good?' Grace wondered.

God tried to think of a way he could answer without betraying his lack of omnipotence but decided he was better off just maintaining an enigmatic silence.

They continued along the street, watching the slow creep of the renovation and keeping their eyes peeled for babies.

# Chapter Twenty-One

COLONEL GERRY TESTED the wind direction and shifted his rifle to a perfect position on his shoulder. Having adopted a lookout position on the raised track of the Leap Frog railroad, he was able to see over a good deal of the park and, using his long-range sight he was now squaring-up for a shot on one of the intruders: a young black woman, dressed in the most awful, tatty clothes. She looked like some form of labourer, he decided: dirty denim trousers and a jersey with strange writing on it. No doubt it was the emblem of the company she worked for. Well, 'Nike' (Greek perhaps?) was about to have one less member of staff on its books. He cocked the rifle, breathed out and tightened his finger on the trigger.

# Chapter Twenty-Two

NEITHER GRACE NOR God knew what the gunshot was until later. The noise was so sudden and the glass lamp above Grace's head shattered with such force that their first assumption was that it had simply exploded.

They both ran to the other side of the midway, Grace hunched over, showered with broken glass.

'Stand still,' God told her. They were stood within the entrance to the Hippodrome Racetrack, a large dirt track arena where once chariot races and parades would have entertained the crowds sat in the tiered seating that surrounded the track. At the centre was a lagoon, its rippling surface reflecting a sky long gone to history.

God began picking the glass out of Grace's hair, shard by shard. 'Don't move,' he told her. 'I don't want you to cut yourself.'

'Oi!' came a voice from across the way. 'You two

shouldn't be here.'

'Great,' said Grace, breathing in sharply as God hooked a piece of broken glass from the neck of her sweatshirt, 'company.'

# Chapter Twenty-Three

COLONEL GERRY COULDN'T have been angrier. He prided himself on the number of shots he'd missed in his life. They could be counted on his one hand. Now, no longer.

'Get off me, you little swine!' he shouted, shaking his leg where one of the babies was clinging on, its tiny teeth embedded in his calf. It had been the baby's bite that had spoiled his aim and now he couldn't get rid of the damned thing.

He beat at it with the butt of his rifle. This didn't seem to cause the baby any pain though it did, finally, release him and scamper away along the racetrack.

He quickly reloaded but held off taking a shot, the thing moved too fast, his ego couldn't take another missed target.

He turned back to where he'd been aiming in the first place but the visitors were now hidden by the cover of the racetrack entrance; there was no clear shot to be had.

As if that weren't bad enough, they also now had company, some of the damned little people from Midget City.

'I'd be better off shooting the whole damn lot of them,' he said, 'clear this place up once and for all.'

It was sorely tempting, though he knew Gloria would give him hell for it. Women, too damn soft, even when they were dead.

# Chapter Twenty-Four

'YOU NEED TO get out,' said Horlicks, looking God and Grace up and down with unashamed loathing. 'Right now.'

He turned to the rest of his sub-team to share in the loathing, then remembered he was here with Fabrizzi and Lucy—well, they couldn't be trusted on their own could they?—who were hardly likely to join in with some righteous anger towards strangers.

'We can't just yet,' said Grace, 'we need to feed the babies.'

'Yes,' said Horlicks, 'the babies. We've seen how well you've handled that task haven't we? I have several sub-teams combing the place as we speak. We'll have them bagged up and back where they belong *eventually*.' He put extra emphasis on this last word, determined to get across how infuriating the situation was. 'In the meantime you two need to get out of the park. Your presence is dangerous and I think we can all agree you've caused quite enough trouble without adding more.'

'Dangerous?' Grace asked.

'The park's waking up,' said Fabrizzi, sidling over to her and adopting what he liked to think was a suitably "cool" pose. Suddenly, a thought occurred to him. 'How old are you kid?'

'Fifteen. Why?'

He sighed. 'You looked older. I never can tell with tall girls.' He stopped posing and just stood up normally. 'The park senses there are punters here, new people, you know, an audience...' He pointed at the two of them. 'So it comes up out of its... hey Horlicks, what's the expression you use?'

'Dormant state,' Horlicks replied. 'It comes out of its dormant state and all the rides and exhibitions come to life.'

'But you're already alive,' said God, 'aren't you?'

Horlicks shrugged. 'Tell you the truth we've kinda given up on that one; dead or alive, who knows what we are?'

'The most handsome thing eyes will ever see,' said Fabrizzi with a wink, 'that's what.'

Lucy jabbed him in the ribs. 'If you were any more bigheaded your neck would snap.' She looked at Grace. 'It really is important you leave.'

'But we can't,' she explained, 'if we walk out of here

without having fed the babies the Queen will kill us both anyway.'

'Well,' said God, pointing at Grace and nodding then pointing at himself and shaking his head. 'But the point still stands. How dangerous is it for you if the park wakes up?'

'Dangerous enough,' said Horlicks, 'but not for long because once you two are dead the park will fall back asleep again and all will be well. So, you know,' he tried to look menacing, 'maybe you can guess the two choices I'm working with here?'

'Leave or we'll kill you,' said God, 'yes. I'm not sure I'll be able to allow that sort of thing but, for now, let's just accept that you've offered your threat and move on shall we?'

'Allow it?' shouted Horlicks, 'is this about size, buddy? Because if it is, let me tell you, I've taken down bigger than you in my time!'

'Horlicks,' snapped Lucy, 'don't get yourself worked up, I'm sure there's no need.' She looked at Grace and God, her face narrowing. 'You wouldn't be so stupid as to be being sizeist would you?'

'You're all my children,' said God.

'He's saying we look like children!' screamed Horlicks and began punching God.

'I wasn't! I wasn't!' God shouted. 'I meant it purely in the biblical sense.'

'He's God,' said Grace.

Horlicks stepped back. 'If he is then I'm definitely happy to beat him up,' he said. But, before he could return for a second round of treating God like a punch-bag, another shot rang out and Horlicks would never punch anything ever again.

# Chapter Twenty-Five

COLONEL GERRY TOOK stock. He had killed one of those damned little people. How did that make him feel? Certainly not guilty. If need be he could tell Gloria that it had been an accident, that the fellow had stepped into the shot at the last minute. Yes. Perhaps he could also tell her that the rest of his diminutive clan wouldn't listen to reason after that, and that he had therefore had no choice but to kill some more of them. Yes. He thought he could say all that quite easily. She might even believe it.

He raised the gun to his shoulder once more.

# Chapter Twenty-Six

'SOMEONE'S SHOOTING AT us!' Fabrizzi wailed, dashing into the cover of the doorway so quickly he all but winded Grace as he collided with her.

'Someone?' said Lucy, joining him at a more controlled pace, 'I think we know who it's likely to be don't we?'

'The crazy colonel you mean?'

'"Crazy colonel"?' God asked.

'Used to be the lion tamer here,' she explained, 'fell in love with a movie actress, died, came back, bit mad.'

'Yeah, well, that's us up to speed,' said God nodding at Grace, 'you need to keep in the loop. Ask more questions.'

'That kind of depends on what happens in the next few minutes, don't you think?' Grace replied as two more shots rang out and the wood of the racetrack entrance gate splintered above them.

# Chapter Twenty-Seven

COLONEL GERRY HAD decided that it didn't count as a miss if you weren't aiming. After all, sometimes it was useful to flush out the prey wasn't it? To force the target into the open where it could be cleanly and swiftly despatched.

Yes. That was constructive and in no way counted towards his missed shots.

He cocked the rifle and fired again.

The entrance to the racetrack was white wood surrounded by electric bulbs. It offered roughly two feet of cover. Less, the more he managed to chip away at it with his bullets. Clearly the gate was closed otherwise they would have gone inside. Once in the seating ring of the auditorium he would be unable to get a line of sight on them but that wasn't a problem as, clearly, they couldn't get in.

Yes. This was actually shaping up rather well.

He took his next shot.

# Chapter Twenty-Eight

'WOULD YOU LIKE to come in?' asked a voice from the other side of the entrance gate. God looked down and gave a shocked yelp as he saw the face of the person on the other side. She was about five foot, wearing bib pants and a loose light blue blouse. Where things got really disturbing, especially for slightly conservative deities, was the head. It was a single, head-sized eyeball.

'I know,' the eyeball said (*But how?* God thought. *Where's its damned mouth?*), 'my appearance can be slightly startling. I do prefer it if people don't scream when they see me though. Yes. All things considered I like it better that way.'

'I'm so sorry,' God replied, 'unforgivable response on my part. Let's start over. Preferably, as you so wisely suggested, on the other side of this gate.'

'No problem,' the eyeball said, 'screaming happens

115

sometimes, I'm not going to pretend it don't.' While she was talking, she was working on the padlock that held the entrance gate closed, two thin strips of metal working away inside the keyhole.

Suddenly, the padlock clicked open, she removed it, opened the gate and stepped inside to let everybody through. Just as Fabrizzi passed through, another bullet ricocheted behind them.

The relief on Fabrizzi's face to be out of harm's way immediately turned sour once he saw the face of his saviour. 'Oh no,' he said, 'the freaks are out too.'

'The freaks,' said the eyeball, 'just saved your life. All three foot of it.'

'Yes!' said Fabrizzi, 'three foot! Thirty-six inches of perfection! As I'm sure you can see quite clearly!'

'Please stop arguing,' said Lucy, she looked at the eyeball. 'Thank you very much Peeper.'

'That's your name?' asked Grace. 'Peeper?'

'Yep,' Peeper agreed. 'Ain't got no surname neither. I guess nobody was willing to admit to it.'

On this side of the entrance gate, there was a small ticket booth to the right, a set of steps leading down to the track straight ahead and, on the left, the first of four rows of bench seating. Peeper pointed at the shadows beneath the bench.

'And this here's my friend Demi-John.'

From out of the shadows appeared the top half of a

handsome, dark-haired boy of about thirteen. There was no bottom half, he was resting on a wooden trolley with casters in each corner.

'Pleased to meetcha!' he said. 'Hope you don't mind if I don't get up.'

This was clearly an old joke, designed to defuse his embarrassment; he didn't laugh and nor did anyone else.

'I guess you must be the two idiots who let the babies out?' he asked.

'Yeah,' Grace admitted. 'I'm Grace and this is God.'

'The one and only.' God gave a small bow.

'God. Right. Of course you are,' said Peeper, 'big fan of your work.'

'Thank you,' God replied, 'though I'm just the one who set the ball rolling, I really can't take all the credit.'

'I'm sorry about your friend,' said Grace, looking through the gate towards the dead body of Horlicks.

'He wasn't exactly that,' admitted Lucy, 'but it's awful to see him like...' She turned away.

Fabrizzi put his arm around her. 'At least it wasn't us,' he said in what he no doubt thought of as a reassuring tone. She gave him a disparaging look and pulled away.

Fabrizzi shrugged and looked at Grace. 'Just trying to help.'

'We need to keep moving,' said Demi-John. 'If the Colonel's decided to shoot us all he'll be on his way soon enough.'

'Why would he want to shoot you in the first place?' asked Grace. 'Ok, I guess I can understand why he thinks it's a good idea to kill me and God but you guys live here.'

'The Colonel's got a few problems,' said Peeper. 'He always was a bit flaky but since we came back... I don't know, it's been weird for all of us, trying to figure out who we are. It's not like the rest of you out there, the world just changed around you, but we're a part of that. I remember my time here but I also remember the life after, when the park burned down and we all went our separate ways. I ended up working a travelling show down south. So how come I'm back here, now, a kid again...?'

'Don't question it!' said Fabrizzi. 'We've been given a second chance! Young and beautiful again!' He looked at Peeper. 'Well, some of us at least.'

'Seriously guys,' said Demi-John, 'we can talk on the way but we need to get out of here.'

'We need to gather up the babies somehow,' said God. 'Once we've done that Grace and I can get out of here.'

'Perhaps we should just leave,' said Grace. 'It's not really fair to endanger everyone else by hanging around.'

God shrugged, picking up the sack of food. 'Your call, but we both know what's going to happen if we step out of here having not done what we've promised.'

'What's in the sack?' asked Demi-John.

'Food,' said God. 'Apples. Flying ones.'

'Of course they are,' said Fabrizzi tapping at his head

in a manner that made it quite clear what he thought of God's state of mind.

'And the babies like them?' asked Demi-John.

'Love them,' said Grace. 'We caught one because it was desperate to eat it.'

'Then I've got an idea that might help, come on!'

# Chapter Twenty-Nine

COLONEL GERRY WAS making his way back down the track of the Leap Frog railway, trying his best not to shout and kick at things. His temper had always been a trifle short. The slightest thing could provoke him, it was what had finally necessitated his withdrawal from the army.

When there had been battles to fight, nobody complained about a soldier with a short fuse; in peace time it became more of a hindrance. That night in India, when he had finally snapped and beaten the slovenly oaf in the laundry room. The damned man never could get a decent crease into his dress shirts.

'You used to pay me to keep the savages in line,' he'd told his commanding officer, 'now you're trying to give me the boot for it.'

'We're not fighting the domestic staff,' the man had said, looking down that fat, blotchy nose of his. 'In fact, now, we're not supposed to be fighting anyone. I'd advise you to take a pension and leave while your reputation is mostly intact.'

And that's what he'd done, resenting every damned moment of it. But the money soon ran out. It was so expensive to live at a decent level these days. The cost of servants, the astronomical rates of travel. He'd earned a reputation handling big game during his time in India so turning it to his financial advantage hadn't been hard, leading safaris, teaching the lily-livered dregs of the colonies to hunt. They paid well and, for a couple of years, he was happier than he ever had been in the army. A loaded rifle and decent savings, what could be better?

Then that damned tiger had taken his hand and the bookings dried up. Nobody, it seemed, quite trusted a big game hunter who had let his prey get too close.

How the mighty had fallen. He had taken the only job he could find, conqueror of empires reduced to public entertainer. They didn't mind his false hand here, no, quite the reverse.

'It gives the audiences a thrill,' Sam Gumpertz had said, 'it reminds them how dangerous the cats are.' Gumpertz was in charge of the acts, he knew a great deal about theatricality but nothing about wild animals. The big cats Colonel Gerry wrangled in the ring were about as dangerous as domestic tabbies. Old and heavily sedated, it was all he could do sometimes to get the damn things to move. Half of his whip work was to keep them awake.

If it hadn't been for Gloria, life would have been entirely miserable. Gloria... if only she had returned to life as he had, not the celluloid dream she appeared as now but the real woman, the warm flesh and blood that had coaxed him through his latter years.

Why had she not come back like the rest of them?

He made his way through the bathing pavilion as a shortcut to the miniature Swiss railway. He felt sure he would be able to find a clear line of sight from one of its rocky promontories, pick the little freaks off one by one. He should have done this from the start, he decided, clean the place up. What were any of them for? The freaks and the wasters? The abominations? Yes. Get rid of the lot of them, clear the place out like they had in India, sweep the dead wood aside and build afresh.

Gloria would understand eventually, he was sure of it.

Together they would take over the park, the quiet, dormant park, and make it a place they could live out their years in, however many that may be—it was so hard to be sure, didn't he have vague memories of dying? Older and wasted, body falling apart... The drink? he thought it may have been the drink...

No. That can't have happened, not if he was here now. A second chance. Yes. The clock wound back to when he had still had Gloria—in whatever form, anything was better than nothing—and life could still be worthwhile.

It was a blessing, that's what it was. A blessing he would defend until he had no more bullets with which to do so.

# Chapter Thirty

'WHERE ARE WE going?' asked Fabrizzi, quite irritated at having to run, it did so crumple his suit.

'Bostock's arena!' shouted Demi-John who had proven extremely speedy on his trolly. It was strapped to him, allowing him to move with ease, vaulting down steps and hopping over obstacles. He propelled himself along with his hands, like a bodyboarder traversing the waves.

'And what do we hope to find there?' God asked. 'Other than lots of animals that will probably try and eat us?'

'Tranquilizers!' Demi-John replied. 'They used them on all the wild animals to keep them doped and slow.'

They re-emerged from the racetrack. Peeper checked for sign of Colonel Gerry before gesturing for them to cross the strip of open ground between the racetrack and the Canals of Venice ride.

'If we can dose the apples,' Demi-John continued, 'then the babies will eat them, be out for the count and we can get them all back under lock and key.'

'I like this boy,' said God, 'he has a good mind.'

'Well,' said Fabrizzi, 'so did Horlicks until the Colonel splattered it all over the ground.'

Lucy punched him on the arm. 'If you haven't got anything good to say then don't say anything.'

Fabrizzi rolled his eyes as if, once again, he was the only person there still in possession of his marbles.

The Canals of Venice ride featured miniature canals and bridges, a chocolate box confection of Venice reproduced in a winding boat ride for lazy New York lovers.

'Is this the quickest way?' asked Grace as they ran alongside one of the trickling canals.

'No,' admitted Demi-John, 'but I'm trying to get us there without putting us in the open too much. The Colonel will be on our heels, just waiting for the opportunity to take a shot.'

The renewal that was affecting the park was starting to make itself felt here too, the gondolas that sailed along the canals were becoming brighter, their gold-paint more brilliant.

'How long before the park wakes up completely?' she asked.

'It's gradual,' said Lucy, 'the last time it happened it was an hour or so before it became really alive.'

'That's still not long,' Grace replied. 'I don't want to cause you more problems..'

'It'll be fine,' said Lucy, taking Grace's hand. 'It's good to help someone out for a change rather than the usual bickering and politics.'

'And sneaking peeks at me whenever you can!' laughed Fabrizzi. 'Don't think I don't notice.'

'This way!' Demi-John shouted, shoving a hidden door open that led out of the Venice ride and into the open air again.

They were on a bumper car track and Demi-John encouraged them out carefully.

He pointed up. 'We have to hope he's not up there because there's no cover until we get to the shooting gallery at the other side.'

'I'll go first,' said God, 'least I can do. After all, it's not as if he can kill me anyway.'

He strolled out onto the track before Grace could argue, strolling casually towards the shooting gallery at the other side.

Halfway across he stopped and turned back to face them.

'Seems cool,' he said.

At that moment, the bumper cars, the renewing energy caused by Grace and God's presence having buffed-up their brightly-coloured exteriors to an amazing sheen, began to move. One, painted a bright red and white check, slammed into God and it was only his quick reflexes that stopped it running him over. As it was, he fell across its front, gripping the rim of the driver's cabin, and was immediately transported in wide circles around the track. The sack of apples dangled from one hand as he gripped on to it.

Grace ran to try to help but all the cars were now moving, all aiming for a different member of the party, eager to bump them to death.

'Get across as quick as you can,' shouted Demi-John, grabbing the rear bumper of one of the cars so that it pulled him along. As it spun to face him, he let go, the momentum sending his trolly rolling across the track where he vaulted the barrier and landed with a clatter on the other side.

'Quick as you can he says,' moaned Fabrizzi, running as fast as his legs could take him. 'Easy for him to say, he's on wheels.'

A black and gold car bore down on him. Lucy, running alongside him, shoved him just seconds before it hit. He tumbled to the ground, grazed but alive.

'I knew you loved me!' he cried, getting back to his feet and jumping over the barrier just after her.

Grace and Peeper were trying to grab hold of God. They looked like bullfighters in the ring, darting one way and then the other as the car spun and shifted direction.

'You need to let go!' Grace shouted to him.

'I should,' he agreed, 'it can't hurt after all.' He didn't look at all convinced.

Peeper jumped into the driver's cab and, with all of her strength, managed to force the wheel so that it drove in a straight line towards the barrier.

'Jump when I say,' she told God. 'The barrier's soft, it should help.'

'Bless you, kid,' God replied, trying to smile beneficently through his whipping beard.

'Now!'

God turned and jumped, winding himself on the barrier but toppling over the other side relatively unharmed, the sack landing on top of him.

The car bounced back and Peeper jumped out, falling to the ground as it turned to face her, speeding forward.

Grace lifted her up and they both toppled to safety just as the car hit the barrier a second time, missing them by moments.

'God does not enjoy the fairground,' said God, fighting to catch a breath, 'it is very stupid.'

# Chapter Thirty-One

Colonel Gerry had watched the last few seconds of all this from the roof of the Venice Canal ride. Hadn't he said that the park would become lethal if the intruders weren't dealt with?

There was no shot to be had, not now they had cleared the track and were beneath the awning on the other side. The angles were wrong and he didn't plan on wasting more bullets.

Where were they going? What was their plan?

He needed to think like a hunter, he needed to track them, anticipate them, trap them.

# Chapter Thirty-Two

GRACE WAS LOOKING at Demi-John's hands; his palms were badly grazed but he waved her away. 'I've had worse,' he said. 'And we haven't got time to fuss. We need to get through the shooting gallery, there's a maintenance door in the rear that will take us into Creation.'

'Creation?' God asked, sure they were heading for familiar, religious grounds.

'A hinky ride that shows you how the world was made.'

God chuckled. 'I'll be the judge of that.'

'Then we're there?' asked Grace.

'Pretty much,' Demi-John agreed. All of the rides have maintenance doors leading between them so the mechanics could wander around out of sight of the punters. We can go from Creation right into Bostock's.'

'Let's get on with it then!' said Fabrizzi. 'The sooner

we've got these two to where they need to be, the sooner we can get back to normal around here.'

Peeper looked around. She was sure she'd seen something moving, a shadow passing over them. Probably one of the babies, she decided, scurrying around on the hunt for food.

They moved into the shooting gallery, unaware that Colonel Gerry was still hot on their trail.

# Chapter Thirty-Three

IN THE SHADOWS beneath the bumper car awning, a flicker of light crackled.

'Oh, my poor, deluded soldier,' it whispered, 'what is to become of you?'

Gloria found it hard moving in the open, slipping from one shadow to the next. If she stayed in the light too long she could feel herself dissipating, fading away to nothing. She had needed to spend a couple of minutes beneath a bridge in the Swiss railway, restoring herself after her dash in the sun between the Japanese Tea Rooms and the safety of the buildings.

She wished she could talk to her dear Colonel, to somehow calm him down and convince him there was no need for what he was doing.

Did he think she wouldn't be watching as he shot that poor man from Midget City? Did he think she cared so little for him that she wouldn't be following him every step of the way?

Perhaps it would have been better for both of them if they had never come back. She remembered how they had drifted apart after the park had closed down. Colonel Gerry lapsing further and further into drink, not knowing how to carry on now his job had once more been taken from him. She'd provided for them of course, hadn't her career blossomed just as his had dwindled? But he didn't like that, did he? Didn't like being "kept" by his actress lover.

She remembered the day she had finally walked away, unable to watch him self-destruct a moment longer. It had all but broken her but she couldn't watch him die, that would be too much to bear.

And now they were back together. Ghosts perhaps, or dreams give form, she didn't know. Didn't care. It was what they had, and, again, her destructive soldier was trying to tear it apart. How she wished he could learn.

Feeling strong for her rest in the darkness, she pushed on, only hoping she might be able to do something before he went too far.

# Chapter Thirty-Four

DEMI-JOHN LED them through the shooting gallery and into the large, domed building that housed Creation. Inside, a circular canal ran for over 300 metres, ferrying a large boat through painted panorama of the biblical history of the world.

'Six thousand years!' God shouted. 'They're saying the world's been here for six thousand years?'

He kicked at a grotesque painted display. 'Read a book you ignoramuses, it's people like you that give me a bad name.'

'Can we keep moving?' asked Lucy, 'I don't care if the world's six thousand years old or sixty…'

'Sixty?' God was beside himself, 'try four and a half billion years! And that's just this planet. The universe is much older, just shy of fourteen billion.'

'Well,' Lucy sighed, 'whatever. I'll think about that long

and hard in all the time I have left to me once the Colonel's shot me.'

'Hmm...' God looked abashed. 'Yes, well, maybe I need to think about my priorities, fair enough. I just get so...' He kicked the display again. 'Creationists make my holy balls itch.'

'Thus spake the Lord,' said Fabrizzi with a laugh.

Demi-John was at the far side of the dome now. he waved Grace over.

'Help me with the door would you?' he asked. 'Handle's just too high for me.'

'Course,' she tried it. It was locked.

'Leave it to me, said Peeper, 'I'm good with locks.'

She reached into the front pouch of her bib pants and pulled out the thin strips of metal she had used earlier on the racetrack gate.

'What's it like out there?' she asked Grace. 'You know, in the real world.'

'Weird,' Grace replied, 'there's really no other word for it.'

'Got to be better than in here though,' Peeper replied, 'me and Demi-John spend most of our days looking after the others and getting nothing but grief for it. You think that maybe, when you go, we could come with you?'

She turned to Demi-John who shrugged. 'Hey, who knows if we even exist beyond this place? Maybe we can't leave?'

'I'm willing to give it a try if you are,' Peeper replied.

'I need to find my brother,' Grace explained, 'he's probably in Rikers prison, or maybe he's not anymore but that's the only place I know where to look so...' she shrugged, 'if you want to come with me then that's fine by me.'

It was weird she thought, how she had spent so much of her life being alone and yet now, when it had all gone to Hell, she was gathering friends faster than ever before.

The lock clicked and Peeper pushed the door open.

'Find your brother, yeah, we can do that. I'm great at looking for stuff!'

'Come on you guys!' Demi-John shouted. 'We're in.'

They stepped through into the rear of Bostock's Arena and were immediately hit by the animal smell. Old straw, meat and dung, all bundled together into something both sweet and nauseous.

'How safe you think this is?' Fabrizzi asked, peering into the shadows.

'This is Dreamland,' Lucy replied, 'nothing is safe these days.'

It was dark and Grace found herself staring at the bars of a small cage containing nothing she could see but shadows.

It hit her suddenly. The cabin. Her home for so long. The place that had nearly been the ruin of her at the same time as saving her from The Change.

The breath caught in her throat and she was back there, back in the cage.

# Chapter Thirty-Five

'IT'S FOR YOUR own good, girl,' said Uncle Ray, turning the long metal key in the lock. 'It's a terrible world out there, full of crazy, godless, devils. I've seen the way they are. I've seen the way they behave.'

Grace said nothing. She knew from experience that no words would turn Uncle Ray from his path. He would lock her in the cage, insist she said her prayers and eventually, when his righteous fury had simmered down a little, he would let her back out.

It's not as if the cage even made much difference, not really. The cabin was miles away from anywhere and he didn't let her use her laptop or phone, not anymore. She was as trapped on one side of the bars as the other. If she kept quiet, kept her head down, he might not hit her and that was the best that could be hoped for.

The stupidity of it all didn't escape her, her stuck in one

cell, her brother in another. What had she done to deserve it?

'If you say your prayers, and say them real good,' Uncle Ray told her, 'I'll let you out in a couple of hours or so. I am not an unreasonable man. I am a man who loves you. I am a man who is willing to do what needs to be done to set you on the path of righteousness, the path that leads to God's love.'

There was no telling what would set him off. A misplaced word, a look in your eye, sometimes Uncle Ray just saw the devil creep in and then you either fought him—and got the belt for your trouble—or you accepted your fate and waited out the solitary confinement here in the 'Cage of Jesus'. It was never for too long, overnight at the worst. You did your time and moved on.

But that day had been different hadn't it? Because that had been the day of The Change. The day the sky had opened up and Uncle Ray had got conclusive proof of the devil he had always known was lurking just out of sight.

He hadn't seen it directly, he'd been praying in the corer of his bedroom, hollering hosannahs to the very heights of Heaven. But he'd seen it later, seen the video of it that had ended up circling the Internet a couple of times before the Feds finally shut it down.

Grace hadn't seen the video of course, Uncle Ray had been quite convinced that even a glimpse of it would 'taint her soul'. In a way, he'd been right.

'Please Uncle Ray,' she begged, 'you've got to let me out now.'

'No, no,' he'd muttered, 'that's the only place you'll be safe.' Then he'd watched the video again, talking to himself as he watched the grainy footage. It must have been caught by a security camera, she guessed, or maybe someone had set their phone to upload automatically, the camera still filming even as its owner died. However it happened, all she knew of its contents was what she could pick up through Uncle Ray's chatter.

'Leviathan,' he whispered, 'bursting from the sky with its dark heart, gazing down on us with its eyes... so many eyes... Judging us good... Judging us ripe...'

When he'd finally died, his body just a few feet from the bars, she'd cried, then screamed, then slept, her brain switching off rather than having to deal with the situation.

She had no idea how long she slept for; she'd slipped in and out of consciousness, sometimes waking in darkness, sometimes in daylight. She'd started trying to shift the bars, then picking away at the wooden floor in the hope of crawling underneath the boards. The key was in her uncle's pocket but, stretching as far as she could, she still couldn't reach him.

She had watched his body bloat then deflate. The smell had made her wretch but eventually either she got used to it or it just went away.

The hunger was the worst. She had water in the cage, several big plastic bottles of it—Uncle Ray would often insist she washed and scrubbed herself with it several times a day to 'cleanse herself of sin'—so thirst wasn't an immediate problem and she had the sense to eke it out as much as she could. Still, she would die in the cage unless she caught a break, she knew that.

That break came when she finally managed to loosen one of the floorboards. With bloody hands, she'd torn it free and peered underneath only to find there was only a few inches space below, nowhere near enough to move through. For a moment, her exhausted, panicked mind had thought that was the end. She finally accepted she would die soon.

Then she'd realised she could use the board for something else. She'd squatted by the bars, poking the board through and slowly, ever so slowly, managed to roll the dead body of her uncle close enough to reach.

Grimacing, she'd searched his pockets, trying not to think about the way his dead flesh gave beneath the cloth as her fingers dug around. Finally the key was in her hand. She unlocked the cage, ran outside and sobbed into the earth of the free world.

It had taken her a little longer to leave the cabin. She'd buried her uncle—his madness might nearly have killed her but she couldn't leave the body—stocked up on provisions and walked out of there.

But at night, ever since, when she dreamed, she was back in the cage and part of her wondered if she'd ever really left it at all.

# Chapter Thirty-Six

'GRACE,' GOD ASKED, putting a hand on her shoulder, 'are you alright?'

She tore her eyes away, pulled herself back from the memory of her own cage. This wasn't it. She wasn't in the cabin. She had escaped. She was sure of it.

'Memories,' was all she could say, turning away and looking around with the rest of them.

'Where do you think they hid the drugs?' asked Peeper. 'There must be a cupboard or something.'

Demi-John pulled himself along the floor but found the going harder here than outside, the straw and dirt catching in his wheels. 'I don't know, keep looking, it must be here.'

'If it works,' said Lucy, 'I mean, most of the things in the park are real, real enough to eat or drink anyway, but what if the tranquillisers aren't like that? What if they don't even exist anymore?'

'Then we've wasted our time,' Demi-John admitted, 'but we might as well try.'

'Has anyone else noticed the smell is getting worse?' asked Fabrizzi. 'It really stinks in here.'

Grace had. 'This place is waking up too,' she said.

A low growl emerged from the shadows of the cage Grace had been looking at.

'The animals,' said God, 'we need to be careful.'

'The animals didn't come back,' said Fabrizzi, 'no idea why. We see ghosts of them sometimes. Even hear them occasionally. They're safe though, they pass right through you. They're not actual, solid, bitey animals. Maybe you had to be human for it to happen.' He adopted a theatrical pose of thoughtfulness. 'Or just breathtakingly gorgeous.'

The low growl became louder and then, from the shadows, a large shape burst into the air. It had been a lion once, perhaps it would soon be one again. For now it was a thing of memory, built from the impressions of those who had thrilled to it in years gone by. 'Mama!' the children had cried, 'look at the size of its teeth!' and those teeth were indeed big, bigger than any naturally born animal. 'Look at the strength in its paws, could take your head off with a single blow!' Oh yes, yes indeed it could. It was the wild animal of fantasy, a nightmare creature as powerful as every flinching spectator and awe-struck passer-by had made it.

It took Baron Fabrizzi's head in its jaws, and left the rest of him behind.

'Fabrizzi!' Lucy screamed, scarcely able to believe what she had just seen. Fabrizzi's stump of a neck spurted once, then twice, then his body—his pride and joy—toppled backwards into the dirt.

'Found them!' Peeper shouted, unaware of what had just happened. She stood at the far side of the room, Demi-John beside her. In her hands was a large glass bottle and some syringes.

When she saw the lion she almost dropped both. 'Oh Lord...'

It paced between them, switching its attention from one side to the other. Would it go for Peeper and Demi-John on one side of the room or God, Grace and Lucy on the other?

'Leave this to me,' said God. 'If I could save Daniel when he was cast into the lion's den, I can certainly save you lot.'

'Don't!' Grace shouted. 'It'll tear you to pieces.'

'I'm God,' he replied, calmly. 'How many times do I have to tell you? God does not get torn to pieces by lions. In fact, God does not get torn to pieces by anything.'

He marched up to the lion, pointed at it and shouted at the top of his voice. 'Shut your mouth you roaring asshole!'

It stared at him, its growl continuing to purr away in its throat like the idling motor of a motorbike.

God turned around and began to walk towards the main entrance. 'We're walking out of here,' he told the lion, 'and you're simply going to go back in your corner and have a nice quiet sleep. I am a kindly and forgiving God so, even though you bit the head off a friend of ours, I will let you live.'

He opened the main door, letting the light flood in. The lion cowered from it slightly, as if scared of the outside world. God turned back to face it.

'But mind me! I will not tolerate you threatening another of my children. They are precious to me and you will obey your creator.'

The lion growled again and then, with a ferocious snarl charged at him.

'I'm telling you!' God shouted, stumbling back into the daylight, 'I won't stand for disobedience.'

The lion leapt into the air, paws spread wide, talons bared.

There was a gunshot and it recoiled in the air, twisting slightly as it collided with God, the pair of them falling to the ground.

'I was perfectly in control,' God insisted, from his position beneath the dead lion.

'Force of habit,' said Colonel Gerry, reloading his rifle, 'I should have saved myself a bullet and let it kill you.'

He pointed his gun at God as the others came running out of Bostock's Arena. 'Never could resist bagging a decent cat,' he said. 'Maybe I'll hang its head on my wall once I've tidied this place up once and for all.'

'Please don't!' Grace shouted, running over to God, who was struggling to free himself. 'We'll leave, there's no need to do this.'

'There's every need,' said Colonel Gerry, 'look around you! Look at the chaos of this ungodly place!'

The whole park was close to wakefulness now, from within the buildings, rides were whooping and rattling along their tracks. The midway was filling with the ghosts of spectators gone by, ethereal figures pointing and laughing at its amusements. A herd of carousel horse, their wooden teeth gnashing even as calliope music burst from their throats, leaped onto the racetrack and began chasing one another.

As the Colonel stared, a baby scurried past his feet, chasing a reanimated roast chicken that squawked and flapped its golden, crispy wings.

'It's disgusting,' he said, 'and any moment now it'll turn on the lot of us.'

From the lagoon there came the sound of rushing water as something massive began to rise from its depths.

'It's everything that was ever wrong with this damned country,' he said, 'it's excess, gluttony, perversion and bad taste.'

On the dome of the Creation ride, the forty foot, marble statue of a naked woman that presided over the Surf Avenue entrance, was pulling herself along, the roof cracking beneath her weight. She opened her cold, empty mouth and roared with the sound of a hundred church organs.

'Disgusting,' Colonel Gerry sighed, 'brazen, whorish, mad. The very worst kind of woman.'

He raised his rifle and curled his finger around the trigger. 'It must all be made to go away. Everything in its right place.'

The flash of light that collided with him was unrecognisable to Grace and God; it was nothing more than a blur of movement that swept him up and whisked him along the midway towards the closest point of darkness: the entrance to the Hell Gate ride.

'What are you doing?' he screamed, the rifle falling from his hands.

He came to land in the shadows. Above the building, a mammoth, leather-winged representation of the devil chuckled and craned its neck to watch.

'It's for the best, my love,' said Gloria, her flickering face adopting a look of pure sorrow. The heat from her as she held him close began to make his clothes singe.

'You're burning me!' he cried.

'I'm burning us both,' she replied, 'back to memory, back to dreams.'

There was a crackle of celluloid and the light burst from her, banishing every shadow in the mouth of the ride. The grotesque barges lined up to take their passengers into the subterranean passages beyond twisted and crackled in the heat. The flames caught and began to curl their way up the tar-painted grotto entrance.

The fire that had once claimed Dreamland, triggered in this very building, was once again blazing.

# Chapter Thirty-Seven

ONE PANIC WAS now replaced with another.

Lucy, still in shock at the sight of Fabrizzi's death realised more would soon follow unless she acted quickly.

'We've got to get everyone out of here!' she said. 'Everyone in the village.'

'And our lot,' said Demi-John, 'we need to run.'

'The babies,' said Grace, 'we can't let them all get burned.'

God, finally dragging himself free from beneath the carcass, pointed towards the far end of the midway where, even now, crowds were erupting from Midget City. 'I don't think that'll be a problem.'

As the residents ran towards the exit, the babies emerged from their hiding places looking up at the flames of the Hell Gate ride and cooing with pleasure.

'Fetch the bag,' he said 'we need to lure them out.'

Grace ran back inside Bostock's, grabbing the sack of apples. She stood by the main exit, untying the knot in the sack just enough that she could snatch one of the apples out. It fluttered in her hand as she held it up in the air.

'Come on,' she shouted, 'dinner time!'

She let the apple go and it hovered in the air for a moment, tiny heads watching it with hunger as it swooped towards the flames and then, with a jolt, retreated towards the exit.

The babies ran for it, bursting from doorways and windows, scampering along the midway, eyes on the apple.

'Plenty to go round,' Grace said, stepping outside the exit and upending the sack. the apples burst into the sky of Coney Island, dipping and swooping like bright red swallows as they explored this new world. Once again, Grace was bowled over as the babies pushed past her and made their own way out into the world beyond Dreamland.

God came running out of the incubation room, the baby he'd caught earlier in his arms.

By now the midway was crowded, everyone forcing their way out of the exit.

'Come on!' Demi-John shouted, 'you're being too slow!'

'I'm moving as fast as I can,' complained Jolly Irene as she dragged herself along behind him with the assistance of Toney the Alligator Boy and Jean Libbera, the latter supporting her with all four of his arms. 'It's hard to run when you're as voluptuous as I am.'

God stepped outside to join Grace and, behind them, their absence was immediately felt. With its audience gone, the park suddenly floundered even as it burned. The racing carousel horses solidified mid-leap and fell lifeless to the ground; the marble woman atop the Creation ride reached towards the sky—perhaps to somewhere she thought of as home—and then toppled forwards, crashing through the roof and into six thousand years of questionable history; the lagoon settled once more, its calmer waters reflecting the flames that climbed higher and higher, reducing the park, once more to history.

Peeper stood at the exit gate, a long procession of dwarfs running past her.

'Come on!' Grace shouted, beckoning to her. 'It's safe, look! Everyone's still here!'

The dwarfs hadn't vanished on leaving the park; whatever the truth of their existence, life clung to them even once they were beyond its influence.

'It's not that,' Peeper admitted, 'well, not just that. It's alright for you but... the way I look... at least in here I fitted in. Mostly... But out there. Where everyone's normal...'

'Normal?' Grace laughed. 'You have no idea.'

# Chapter Thirty-Eight

'So,' SAID THE Queen, shifting slightly on her throne, though through tiredness or wind it was hard to tell. 'I sent you to feed the babies but, in the end, you thought it best to flood my Queendom with everyone that was living in the park and then burn the place to the ground?'

'Cool stew,' chuckled Corman.

'It wasn't quite like that,' said Grace, 'things got a bit out of control.'

'The fire didn't,' Corman assured his Queen. 'The only thing that burned was the park itself, the flames wouldn't spread beyond it.'

'That's something,' the Queen admitted. 'I'd have been real pissed if you'd set fire to us all.'

'But she didn't,' said Corman. 'In fact she solved your Dreamland problem once and for all.'

'Will you stop sticking up for her damn it!' the Queen

shouted. The sudden loud noise made her head hurt even more than normal. 'OK, whatever, you did a cool thing. I'm happy. See?' She looked up at Grace and God who were rocking gently from side to side on the inflatable floor in her throne room, her face the perfect mask of misery. 'I am the happiest woman alive. Take your damn boat and my permission to travel as far as Rikers.'

'Thank you, Your Majesty,' said Grace, bowing.

'Yeah,' said God, 'thanks a bunch. Consider yourself blessed.'

'I sure will, honey,' the Queen replied, 'just as soon as you weirdoes leave.'

# Chapter Thirty-Nine

THEIR BOAT WAS moored at Coney Island Creek. It was small but big enough for four with extra storage room for equipment, provisions and spare gas for the motor.

'We need to call her something!' said God as he admired it from the shore. Peeper was clambering unsteadily aboard, Demi-John being carried between her and Grace.

'Have I told you how well I can swim?' Demi-John asked. 'The answer is "not very well", you know, just in case I hadn't actually mentioned it.'

'You'll be fine,' said Peeper. 'If we get in trouble I'll help you, haven't I always?'

'How about the *Baron Fabrizzi*?' Lucy suggested, looking up at God, a sad smile on her face. 'He was an arrogant pig, but not a bad man for all that. He'd have loved to have a boat named after him.'

God smiled and nodded. 'The *Baron Fabrizzi*, that's an

excellent name for a boat.' He sat down on the grass next to her. 'You sure you don't want to come with us, it'll be fun!'

'It'll be terrifying,' she replied with a laugh, 'so no, I'd rather stick around here. The Queen's set us up with rooms. Everyone's being terribly nice.'

'Good,' God put his arm around her. 'You have reached your promised land my child.'

'I don't know about that, but it'll do for now. From what I hear it's better than most of the city. Have you heard about Queens? Nobody will go anywhere near there.'

'Yes,' said God. 'I have heard about Queens, it's all anyone seems to go on about. I'm sure it can't be that bad.' He stood up. 'Perhaps we'll visit it on our travels.'

'Maybe I should stay here too?' said Demi-John as he pulled himself towards the prow of the boat. 'I think you guys are going to be the death of me.'

'We've already died once,' said Peeper, sitting down next to him, 'what's once more?'

God clambered unsteadily aboard, dropping down on the bench at the stern with such force everyone had to hold on to something to stay upright.

'What?' he asked as everyone stared at him. 'God does not normally do boats. He'll get used to it.'

Grace untied the moor rope and started the motor, they waved goodbye to Lucy and the *Baron Fabrizzi* began its journey westward towards the Hudson.

'Hey,' announced God, ruffling in his robes, 'has anyone seen my bottle?'

'Bottle?' Grace asked.

'It's OK,' he said, pulling an infant's feeding bottle from his sleeve, 'I've got it.'

Grace sighed. 'You didn't...'

'Didn't what?' God asked pulling the baby he'd rescued from the incubator room out of his other sleeve and offering it the bottle.

'You kept one!'

'Well,' he said, 'I didn't like to abandon her. She seems to have taken to me.' This was true, the baby hanging off his arm and giggling, steadfastly ignoring the offered bottle. 'Besides,' he added, 'she'll be safer with me. God doesn't really do danger.'